Yesterday's Battles

Yesterday's Battles

Jack Whyte

IGUANA

Copyright @ 2020 Jack Whyte
Published by Iguana Books
720 Bathurst Street, Suite 303
Toronto, ON M5S 2R4

Front cover design: Meghan Behse
Cover image: Jack Whyte

ISBN 978-1-77180-430-1 (paperback)
ISBN 978-1-77180-431-8 (epub)
ISBN 978-1-77180-432-5 (Kindle)

This is an original print edition of *Yesterday's Battles*.

Contents

To Beverley

Foreword

For several years now, ever since my doctor advised me to forget about buying green bananas and put my affairs in order instead, I've been experimenting with short forms of fiction that, for years, I had left unexplored. I don't know why that was. It may simply have been because my publishers, throughout the world, were predominantly top-tier, traditional houses that published "big" books. For upwards of two decades, then, on both sides of the millennium, I researched and wrote a string of hefty novels that included two trilogies and the four concluding novels of the nine-volume Arthurian cycle, set in Roman Britain in the late fourth and early fifth centuries, that is known in Canada as *A Dream of Eagles* and in the US as *The Camulod Chronicles*.

Then, faced suddenly in 2017 with the strong probability of imminent death, I was forced to choose between continuing to write as I had before—which would entail more years of research than I might be able to handle—or tackling another form of writing altogether, that indistinct, hazily defined form I had never understood and always avoided: short fiction, or the world of short stories and novellas.

With the exception of a single period when I was physically and mentally debilitated and unable to write at all, it never once crossed my mind that I might simply give up writing entirely. Plenty of time to stop writing, I remember thinking, once I've stopped breathing.

It didn't take long for the pleasures and the challenges of writing in the new format to kick in: I quickly discovered the practical importance of brevity, tension, terseness, tightness of focus, and shorter word counts, all dictated by the enormous discipline entailed in switching from long, discursive narrative to tight, succinct storytelling. Both forms have their own rules and rigours, and both demand the same expertise and skill: the deceptively easy-looking techniques of using and manipulating the nuances of our magnificently complex language to generate structure that is silken and transparent in its smooth integrity.

But where to begin?

That was a tough one, because I had no idea of where I actually wanted to go. I found—and sometimes I *still* find—the prospect of "shortness" intimidating, never having felt a need to constrain the free-wheeling narrative style that I had developed over a lifetime. Reorienting myself to work with greater focus in order to say as much with fewer words was, almost instantly, an existential dilemma for me. How could I abandon all my stylistic quirks and still remain the writer I had been? I fretted about that for months, beating myself up, until I remembered a short story that I had written years earlier for a long since defunct American publication called *Paradox*, a magazine of speculative and historical fiction. It was the only short story I had ever written, and I wrote it because I was intrigued at the time by how the kernel of the tale had first occurred to me. And it had actually been published! And long afterwards, just before I fell ill, someone had wanted to reprint it, though nothing ever came of that because other things came to usurp my attention about then.

I dug up that story and read it, and was surprised to discover that it held together remarkably well for a one-off side trip. I took the time to analyze it, paying attention to what made it work, and quickly realized that it worked for precisely the same reason that my novels worked: it brought its characters instantly to life, presenting them as credible and, above all, genuinely human. And so I decided to have another go at short stories.

Since then, I've been beavering away happily again, confident in what I have done in creating this collection, and that original story,

"Power Play," is part of it. I have discovered, to my absolute, unanticipated delight, that this "new" medium is one to which I've been able to adapt with far more ease and mental satisfaction than I had ever thought possible, and the result is a growing collection of new material, far different from anything I've done in the past—a new body of work I'm looking forward to publishing.

This particular collection came into being because I realized that, in the course of a long and fortunate career as an internationally published author, I had never written about my boyhood in Scotland in the 1940s and '50s. The more I thought about that, the more strangely disloyal it seemed, and as my boyhood memories returned to me, sometimes with stark clarity, I began to discern how several seminal moments had influenced the man I later became. Since then, in writing these stories and revisiting the memories that kick-started them, it became clear to me that I had been indelibly influenced by several recurrent notions and preoccupations that I had never recognized were there inside me.

I came to realize that the Elysian Fields I played in as a boy—vast tracts of cultivated, manicured acres that we took for granted and thought of, simply, as "the Estates"—were among the twentieth century's last remaining traces of the society of aristocrats, known as the landed gentry, that had, for hundreds of years, deemed our families to be beneath them: the working classes, unfit to pass through their privileged gates except as menial servants. And even then, it was not until much later that I became aware that common working people had no rights in the face of that same sense of entitlement and privilege: no working man's word had any validity against the laws governing property or trespass; working people, at the end of the Second World War, still had to do as they were told, and I remember seeing, in 1944, the intolerant, patriarchal old laird whose dilapidated manor house was far fallen into tree-screened decay less than half a mile from our house lash his whip across one of his farmhands who had not been quick enough to open the gate for the old man's pony and trap. "Old Cummy," as he was known (for Cummings), was typical of the local power brokers who owned the surrounding lands and employed working-class policemen to safeguard both their privileges and their prejudices. And so, decades later, I found myself consumed with the idea of power and how it can be exercised tyrannically by small numbers of self-serving people manipulating others on a grand scale in order to protect their own narrow interests.

Working-class people, for example, were banned from first-class railway travel in those days. Working-class people didn't register in the awareness of the governing classes. They simply couldn't win at anything significant until they experienced two successive world wars and returned home from each of them only to discover that nothing had changed and their sacrifices were largely perceived as useless, taken for granted by their so-called betters. Only then, like the angry Samson, did they mobilize twentieth-century socialism and use it to pull the entire patriarchal edifice down around them in ruins, in Scotland, anyway. But as recently as the early 1950s, the same old rules applied: in religious matters, in the administration of criminal justice, in banking, in school segregation, in dress and deportment, and in the carefully engineered "sectarian violence" fostered by leaders on both sides to keep Protestants and Catholics constantly and increasingly at odds with one another. All of these things were endemic to the class system practised in Scotland—and throughout Britain, if the truth be told.

One of the most telling condemnations I ever heard on that topic of class distinction was voiced by the actor Michael Caine. He had been receiving plaudits from a TV interviewer on *60 Minutes* for his standout performance in the movie *Zulu*—his first major film role— as the young lieutenant who received the Victoria Cross for his heroic defence of a river ford called Rorke's Drift, on the border of Natal and Zululand, where he rallied a tiny garrison of 137 men to withstand a 4,000-strong force of Zulu warriors in the Anglo-Zulu War of 1879. Caine said that the situation was ironic, because had the movie been filmed in the UK, he would never have been allowed, as a common Londoner with a Cockney accent, to play the role of Lieutenant

Gonville Bromhead. And there, in a nutshell, he encapsulated the suffocating, pretentious hypocrisy of the British class system and the powers of perception, patronage, and paternalism it was established to defend. The mantra of that system, "Do as you're told," is the very antithesis of "Here, let me show you."

That paternalism, combined over centuries with the British mythical stiff upper lip and dour Scots-Calvinist puritanism, generated in Britain, and far more noticeably in Scotland, a national inability to express emotion or to display love, warmth, or affection, even among close family members. Anger and resentment were easy. Love or tolerance, not quite so simple. The alienation between fathers and sons is a time-honoured trope in literature, but nowhere, I believe, has it ever come close to depicting the total lack of overt affection, or even visible paternal pride, that existed in the Scotland wherein my friends and I spent our boyhood. For affection, understanding, and real companionship in the late 1940s and early 1950s, all of us, without exception, turned away from our families and looked outside. Not much has changed today in that regard; the old rules hold true everywhere. But I'd still bet the farm today, fifty years later, that it's worse where I came from than it has ever been where I am now.

That's where all these stories sprang from, and I had no idea they were ready to emerge. I wrote them remembering the way things had been in my own boyhood, and the more I recalled, the deeper I dug and the more conscientiously I wrote. And now all those themes, memes, and dreams are no longer locked inside me. They are out in the open, in this collection, because every story in here had its genesis, one way or another, in wartime and postwar Scotland.

I hope you'll enjoy them. I'll have more for you soon.

Jack Whyte
Kelowna, BC, Canada
July 2020

Power Play

The seed that generated this story, set in the ancient Rome that motivates my creative Muse more than any other venue or time period, was planted during my mid-teens in Scotland, when one of the members of my high school English class, who typified the kind of snooty, pontificating jerk that everyone loves to detest, came home from a weekend camping trip with some evidently benighted, moronic neo-Nazi friends and presented me (at third hand) with my very first conspiracy theory—which he presented as well-documented, undeniable fact—that a secret international cabal of Jewish bankers controlled the fiduciary affairs of the entire world. Even at the age of fifteen I knew better than to believe that or to let it pass unchallenged, and so I got into one of the few serious blood-drawing fist fights of my youth.

I never really thought about it again until the summer of 2009, when I heard another Scotsman spout the same unconscionably racist bigotry that had disgusted me so many years earlier. This time, though, the speaker was someone who, in my opinion, should have known much better and should have kept what were to us his unsuspected prejudices tightly stifled.

We had been talking idly over a cold beer that day—it was summer and we'd been playing golf—first about the trappings and then about the reality of power and how people perceive it and achieve it, and that's when the garbage erupted. This time, however, instead of fighting over it, I wrote the piece that follows.

They were everywhere, Levi thought, everywhere he looked and everywhere he could not see. Romans. The entire country was in their grip, a pigeon in the mouth of a cat.

He turned away from the window, with its view of the drab, brown-clad legionaries on parade across the street, and looked back towards the man seated behind the table with his neat piles of rolled parchments. In the dust-covered street, a donkey brayed, its ugly hacking cough close enough and loud enough to cover even the sounds of the hawkers and peddlers.

Levi waited for the noise to subside, conscious of the deep stillness within the chamber. The only motion in the room was a mere suggestion: a stationary dance of dust motes in the one beam of bright light that blazed through the window, painting a bright slash across the floor and illuminating a corner of one rug and the edge of the table. Surrounding the shimmering brilliance of the sharp-edged swath, the rest of the room seemed dark.

It was a bare chamber, yet sumptuous. Two chairs faced the table side by side, and they were plain and uncomfortable high-backed sellae with their narrow, restrictive arms. A third chair, behind the table, was a curule, the classical Roman magisterial chair, backless, with a polished hide seat supported by curved cruciform ivory legs. The table itself, fully three paces in length, was made of solid slabs of citrus, the rarest and most expensive wood in the world, and the floor was one enormous, brilliantly coloured mosaic. One of the three rugs scattered casually on the floor was obviously Persian, its colours muted yet glowing still despite their antiquity, while another was from the fabulous Eastern Lands, silken and rich with vibrant blues and brilliant reds and yellows. The third was the entire skin of a gigantic white bear. Cured in such a way that its enormous head remained intact, this fantastic creature glared up from the floor directly in front of the table, its gaping jaws revealing teeth as long and thick as Levi's fingers. Two marble busts, beloved of the idolatrous Romans, stood on plinths against the wall behind the table, flanking the man who sat in the ivory curule chair. He was leaning forward with his arms crossed, watching Levi closely, a small frown creasing his brow.

"You look amused, Master Levi. That's the last thing I might have expected from a man who has failed to live up to his word and now sits before me as a delinquent debtor. Did I say something humorous?"

Levi sighed. "No, Caius Tullius. You did not. That is not within your capacity."

The frown deepened instantly to a scowl. "What is that supposed to mean?"

Levi stepped forward and sat in one of the high-backed chairs. "It was not supposed to mean anything. It was a plain statement of fact, no more. I believe humour is alien to your nature, that is all." His eyes were fixed on the sunbeam that stabbed through the gloom. "Look at the way the dust motes seem to dance in that beam of light."

The other man's eyes flicked towards the slanted golden column, then returned to Solomon Levi, betraying a spark of anger. "Have you heard even one word of what I have been saying to you, Master Levi?"

"Oh yes. I have heard and absorbed every word, including those you did not say." The other man blinked. Levi clasped his hands over his flat stomach, interlacing his fingers. "Would you like me to repeat them? Or the sense of them as I understood them?"

Tullius's head dipped sideways. "I would. I would indeed. Please. Surprise me."

"You have been telling me," Solomon Levi said, "that you are about to terminate my livelihood, casting me and all who depend on me into destitution, and inviting me to believe that you have no choice in the matter."

The Roman's eyebrows rose. "Did I say that?"

"Yes. Not in those precise words, but we both know that is what you've been saying for the past hour."

"I see. Then why are you not angry?"

Levi stifled a sigh. "Why should I be angry? What would I achieve? There is nothing I can do to stop you, other than by acceding to your demands for more money, and I am powerless to do that."

"Ah! Powerless. I see." Tullius looked away, his gaze drifting towards the window and the street outside. "Tell me, Master Levi, do you understand what power is, what it represents?"

"Of course I do. It represents itself, for itself, by its very existence. I also know enough about it to know I am powerless to influence your evident decision."

The straying eyes snapped back to Levi. "What decision? What have I decided? I spoke of no decision."

"Words, Caius Tullius! Your words, spoken or not, would be pointless and specious in this instance. You did not use them, admittedly, but you had no need of them. Your nature speaks for you." Levi rose to his feet. "I have no time for this. Enjoy your victory, Caius Tullius, before your mouth fills with the taste of the ashes you have just acquired. I must pay off my men, as far as I am able, and see them settled as well as I can before I conclude my affairs here and move on. Good day to you." He moved towards the door.

"Wait!"

Levi half turned. "Why? There is no more to be said."

"Perhaps not. But please, sit. Permit me to think for a moment."

As Levi resumed his seat, his face expressionless, Tullius got up from his own chair and crossed slowly to the window. He was a handsome man, tall and still young enough to look youthful, although the weight of his responsibilities was beginning to show itself in the stoop of his wide shoulders and the slight but clearly graven lines on his face. Levi's eyes missed nothing of the man, noting that the price of the clothes he wore so casually could have sheltered and fed whole families of the city's poor for months.

"You are a strange man, Solomon Levi. One, I suspect, with few equals among those supposed to be your peers. I am tempted to . . . be lenient with you." He swung away from the window, returned to his chair at the table, and looked Levi straight in the eye. "I almost said 'to appease you.' Now why would I wish to say that?" He paused, then resumed in a brisker tone. "On the matter of the moneys, unfortunately there is little I can do. As you so aptly pointed out, I, too, like every other man, have my masters, to whom I am accountable. On some of the other matters, however, we may be able to arrive at a compromise."

"Such as?"

"We'll come to that. But there will be a price."

The merest hint of a smile touched Levi's lips, then vanished. "There always is. But I have no more money."

"I did not mean money. The price will be some of the contents of your mind. Payable immediately."

"My thoughts, you mean? Interesting. And for what... commodity will I be paying?"

"Understanding. *My* understanding." Tullius watched him. "That makes you smile. Why?"

Levi shook his head slightly. "Simply because of your need to believe that I have any need of your understanding. You Romans value understanding, Caius Tullius. Few others do—particularly in this land of ours. But Romans crave it. You lust after it, are obsessed by it. Why? Can you not simply accept that there are some things that defy understanding? Or that knowledge, in and of itself, is enough? Why are you driven to *understand* everything?" He brushed the matter away with a flick of his hand. "Fruitless to discuss that. Unless your understanding would permit me to continue with my craft—and you have already said you are powerless to influence that—then I have nothing to gain from any understanding you might have of me. But I confess I am curious nonetheless. About what would you have me speak? What portion of my mind interests you?"

Tullius stretched out his arm idly and thrust his hand into the beam of sunshine that now laid a brilliant band across the table. The hand leapt into prominence, painted with golden light. "The different part," he said, turning his hand and admiring the play of light and shadow as it moved. "The part that makes you able to absorb what I have been saying to you, make a decision based upon it—a swift, drastic decision that radically alters your entire life—and allows you to remain outwardly unruffled as though you had not a care in the world. Those are Roman attributes. One does not expect such—what is the word? Sophistication, I suppose—from . . ."

"From a Hebrew?"

"From one who is not Roman, was my thought."

"A barbarian."

"A non-Roman."

"Not of the blood."

"What blood? Roman blood?" Tullius smiled. "There is no longer any such thing, Levi, you know that. The ideal did exist, once upon a time, when wealthy patrician Roman families took pride in being descended from Romulus and Remus. But it is more than a hundred years now since the so-called emperor Caracalla decreed that all free men in the empire, along with their wives, were to be awarded full Roman citizenship. That immediately made nonsense of the idea that *anyone's* blood could seriously be considered Roman. So I have no hidden reason for requesting your opinion, merely curiosity."

"What is it that you want to hear?"

The Roman gazed at him through narrowed eyes. "You said earlier you have an understanding of power, and you've shown me the power you have over yourself. Where most men would be raging, or crushed, or emotionally overwhelmed by the situation you now find yourself in, you remain completely calm. Placid. Is that your understanding of power, Solomon Levi? That it is the power of self-control?"

Levi's expression was set and solemn. "Why should you care what I think of power, Caius Tullius, and why should I indulge your urge to know my thoughts?"

Tullius shrugged. "I care what you think because I see that you *can* and *do* think, Solomon Levi, and that in itself is unusual among the clients with whom I deal. Many of my clients function very well within the limited areas they choose to work in, and many have abilities that sometimes verge upon the uncanny in the matters of their trades, but there are very few I would ever think of as being *thinkers*. You, I perceive, are a thinker—a man who uses his powers of logic and deduction to govern his actions. And so I am interested in your opinion."

"But that is ludicrous, Caius Tullius. I am a simple man, a craftsman. I have no wealth, no sophistication, as you so pointedly observed a moment ago, and I certainly have no power. The fact that I am here, at your bidding, at your mercy and at your disposal, demonstrates that, does it not? Why do you seek to humiliate me by asking me what I know about power?"

"Few equals among your supposed peers, I said. I take that back. It was inadequate and ill considered. You have no equals, and I am disappointed in myself not to have seen that before now. I called you here as a recalcitrant debtor, an unknown, delinquent nuisance to be dealt with firmly. But instead I find an opponent to be reckoned with—a client with a mind." He rested his elbow on the arm of his chair, leaned his weight on it. "So be it. No more false modesty from you, Solomon Levi, and no more blind prejudice from me. Your speech alone, the way you hold yourself, your lack of fear of me and what I represent, all signify your sophistication. Now, again, tell me what you know of power. *All* of what you know."

Levi shrugged in a way that no Roman could ever mimic with authority. "My grandsire's grandsire used to say, 'Be careful what you wish for, lest your wish be granted.' Very well, then. What I have to say may turn you from an importunate moneylender into an implacable enemy, Caius Tullius. But then, since I know you are already such a foe—even though you may not yet realize it—I have nothing to lose by telling you what you wish, or do not wish, to hear."

He stood up and stretched out his hands for Tullius to inspect. "Look at these." They were big hands, dwarfing Tullius's own, their palms hard-skinned and callused, with strong, thick, blunt thumbs and fingers, all with broken nails. "I am a builder. There is power in these hands, you agree? And in these arms," he added, pulling up the sleeve of his robe to display powerful forearms corded with heavy muscle. "Look." He stepped behind the table and, using only one hand, picked up one of the heavy marble busts by the neck, clamping his fingers around it easily. It rose as though weightless, and there was no sign of strain in any part of him. Tullius's eyes widened slightly as he watched Levi replace the statue gently on its plinth and return to the front of the table.

"That is one kind of power, the kind you expect of men like me, no?" He shook his head. "But no. It is a spurious power, without substance, because without moving from your chair you could summon soldiers and have my arms and my hands broken into so many pieces I could never use them again for anything. What is the use of such power to a working man, except for lifting things? It even works against him, because it is useful to you and your like who can threaten to remove it by force, crippling him and leaving him truly powerless. So physical strength is not often worth much to its owner, is it? Where, then, *is* power?"

He waved an arm to indicate the chamber and its furnishings. "This room represents power, all on its own. When I came in, I was led in by a slave who never raised his eyes to look at me, yet let me know by his demeanour that I was less significant than he because he belonged here, whereas I had been ordered to attend. And then I was left waiting, left to be daunted by the richness of this chamber and to become aware of my own lack of worth. Consider that table at which you sit so grandly. Possession of that single piece would finance my entire enterprise and wipe out my indebtedness to you. That is as magnificent a piece of citrus wood as I have ever seen, but then, I have only ever seen three pieces. Yet I would be prepared to wager, in defiance of my creed, that it is as magnificent a piece as you have ever seen, too, no? And you—you are magnificent in your clothes and in your appearance and in your carriage. That too is power, is it not?

"But let us remain with the table. Your table is a symbol of power on its own, quite apart from its value or its substance. This table represents power in its very appearance. Look at it! All that flat, polished, empty space, waiting to be used for momentous things. And the parchment scrolls, so fine, so tightly rolled. So substantial! They are obviously very important documents, otherwise why would they be so carefully rolled and stacked so neatly? Who else but a financier, a merchant who deals in money, would ever take the trouble to roll parchment so tightly, so neatly, so impressively? And to treat each one with such care? And look, only one pen! Only one ink horn. This is the table of no ordinary man. This is the table of a man of power, and every lesser man who sits, supplicant, in one of these lesser, less comfortable chairs, facing this table, is aware of that. These are the trappings of power.

"And when you entered and sat in the curule chair behind the table, I knew who you *are*! Not to mention *what* you are. I wonder, however, whether *you* realize fully who and what you are."

The noises in the street outside hardly seemed to penetrate the room. Tullius stirred. "Go on. I'm enthralled. Who, and what, am I?"

Levi gazed steadily back at the man behind the table. "Are you sure you want an answer to that? Do you not feel the slightest stirring of unease?"

"Yes to the first question and no to the other—not the slightest stirring of unease. Not at all. Should I?"

Levi shrugged his big shoulders. "Who knows? Tell me later. For now, I have to speak of power. I grew up in a village where the second most powerful man in the place—the *second* most powerful—was a carpenter called Ichabod. He was a bad carpenter and always had been, but in his youth, he married a woman called Mehitabel, and she bore him fourteen daughters. Fourteen! And not one son. He was a laughingstock, and perpetually impoverished. But his girls grew and worked hard to lessen their parents' burden, and lo and behold, as they ripened, they grew astoundingly beautiful, each of them a pearl beyond price, as the saying goes, although none of them *was* beyond price. Ichabod sold them off wisely, marrying each to the highest bidder, one after the other. He accumulated a fortune, and he bought land and cattle, and his fortune multiplied. He became a power among our people because he grew rich, and those who had laughed at him soon grew to envy him.

"And one day Ichabod's goats—by this time he had hundreds— attracted the attention of a richer man, from a nearby town, who ruined Ichabod simply because he was both jealous of him and richer than him, and was therefore able to ruin him. Ichabod killed himself, a great sin. By our village standards, you see, Ichabod was powerful, but by the other man's standards, he was weak, because his power— his knowledge, his wisdom—was not great enough to protect either him or itself.

"So you see, riches do not constitute power—unless, of course, those riches are so massive that they become unassailable and inexhaustible, and by that time they have changed. They are no longer merely riches. They have become wealth, and wealth is an entirely different creature. Few men can accumulate real wealth unassisted in one lifetime."

He squinted towards Tullius, whose face was half-obscured in shadow. "And that, I can see you thinking, is ludicrous. Of course they can. And they do. You have done it, have you not? Whereas I, I have not. Therefore your power over me is so absolute that I will not allow it either to surprise me or to anger me." He stretched his own hand into the beam of light. "There. I have told you all you want to hear."

"I think not." Tullius clapped, and the doors opened instantly. "Wine," he snapped to the slave on the threshold, then immediately raised his hand to detain the man, glancing at Levi. "Will you have some? Or is it against your beliefs?"

"It is." Levi smiled. "But it is a lesser sin, a gentle weakness, in moderation. I will have some wine."

The slave departed and Tullius sat for a moment, staring at Levi. "Your thinking interests me, Solomon Levi. Your logical processes. As I said, you are a far more intuitive man than anyone would guess from your appearance. But I think you are still not telling me what you truly believe. You're holding something back, some understanding, or some conviction. Why? Do you judge me unworthy of hearing it because I am Roman?"

Levi laughed, a great, booming sound. "Unworthy, as a Roman? No, not at all!"

"Then why? Believe me, you may be open with me. This is between us alone. Your words, no matter how incendiary, will go no further than this room. If you do not judge me unworthy, then you do consider me an enemy. You have said so. Yet I sense no hatred in you."

Levi shook his head slowly. "You sense no hate in me because I do not hate you, Caius Tullius. I do not even dislike you. You and I could never be friends, but our hostility is intellectual only. I know your *function*, you see—although you do *not* see—and I can appreciate it without admiring it, or condemning it, other than in principle."

"What do you mean, you know my function?"

The slave returned at that point, and they sat in silence until he had poured each of them a glass beaker of wine from a magnificent glass flagon and departed, leaving the flagon on its salver on the table.

Levi raised his cup, sniffed appreciatively, and sipped. "That is delicious. And, of course, you are correct. There is something I am not saying. But you do not wish to hear what else I have to say."

"Try me." Tullius sipped at his own wine.

"So be it." Another sip, then Levi stood up. "Here we are, you in your curule chair behind your table, me standing here. If I were to point now to the power present in this room, where would I point?"

Tullius blinked. "At me."

"Correct." He sipped again. "Now, a suggested change of circumstance." He sat down in his high-backed sella. "Were you to come around and stand here"—he pointed to the chair next to his and waited while Tullius stood up and moved to stand beside him—"can you show me where the power in the room is now, with you standing and me sitting? Where would I point?"

"At me."

"Wrong."

Tullius stood stock-still, a frown clouding his face. "How can it be wrong?" he growled.

Solomon Levi pointed at the empty curule chair behind the table. "Because the power resides there, in that chair, behind this table. When you left it, you left the power behind you. Standing on this side, you are no more than a man, and you are powerless over me."

Tullius scowled. "That is ridiculous."

"You see?" Levi said tonelessly. "I was correct. You did not want to hear it."

Tullius strode around the table and threw himself into his chair. "How could you even say such a thing? I had been listening to you with respect, Levi, but that is ludicrous. Laughable. Stupid!"

"Is it? Where did your personal wealth come from?"

"What concern is that of yours?"

"None, but you are young to have so much of it. You inherited it, did you not?"

"So?"

"So it is not yours." Levi's voice was hard, quite suddenly, and cold. "It belongs to your family, and they accord you the use of it, *providing you do as you are told*. That is your *function*!" The words hung in the air with the dust motes in the sunbeam. In a softer voice, he continued. "I know your family, Tullius. I know your clan. I know far more than you, or any of them, could suspect. If you were to demonstrate an unwillingness, or an inability, to carry out the wishes of your immediate family and their advisors, you would be removed from your post, no? That is why you said there was nothing you could do about the moneys. You are a functionary. The real decisions are out of your hands. Beyond your power.

"You *sit* upon the real power. That chair. Because—and let us be truthful here—that chair represents, along with every other inanimate thing in this room, the truly incredible power that your *family* has accumulated over centuries, a wealth so colossal that its limits are indefinable. It is not *your* wealth, it is your *family's* wealth. It is so enormous that no one person could own it or administer it, although there will always be one paterfamilias charged with the responsibility of administration. But even he will be removed immediately should he ever give cause for concern. Because the power of your family's wealth is so vast that it demands strict patterns of behaviour from the people of the entire world to keep that power functioning. It demands the most rigid *stability* to keep the empire's financial affairs from plunging into chaos. And that need for stability carries within it the awful potential for overwhelming destruction, for annihilation, for unprecedented cataclysmic changes that will accommodate predetermined change. And the responsibility for that pursuit of stability to maintain the wealth resides in the family, in the clan, in the bloodline. And no one who is not of the blood can be allowed to know that truth, because the realization would bring destruction on the clan, and chaos to the entire world."

Caius Tullius was ashen, and his mouth worked aimlessly before he could articulate his next words. "How can you *know* this? Who told you this?" He looked crushed, physically wilted, and his voice sounded as though he had aged thirty years.

Levi emptied his cup and placed it on the ground by his foot. "No one told me. I worked it out for myself, when I was old enough to wonder why people like my father, and like me, and people far greater than either of us, could not survive without the support of people like you, the great moneylenders, even though God had qualified them to do what they do so well. So I began to ask questions. And I listened. And I read. And I looked carefully around me and asked more questions. And eventually I began to discern the beginnings of some answers that conformed, quite frighteningly, to the observations that had led to my questions."

"'Conformed quite frighteningly,'" Tullius said, almost in a whisper. "Explain that, please?"

Levi picked up his empty cup. He rolled it gently between his palms as he spoke. "When I was a boy, I overheard a conversation between my father and one of his greatest friends, a man I had always considered fabulously rich and powerful. That man said something that day that astounded me when I considered it later. Not merely later that day but throughout my life. He said that there are people in this world who are so staggeringly wealthy, and therefore so immensely powerful, that the laws that govern ordinary men do not apply to them, and further that the mass of ordinary men are not only unaware of this, but remain completely unaware throughout their lives that these people exist.

"Years later, when I was afire with the need to *know*, I went back to ask this man to explain what he had meant, but he had died years earlier, taking his knowledge with him. But from the moment I began to form my questions, *I knew there were others who knew the answers.*"

"And what were your questions?"

Levi grinned. "The one in my mind now is: 'Why isn't this man screaming for help and having me thrown into a dungeon as a raving madman?'" He shrugged. "My questions were legion, and they all terrified me because every one of them contained a challenge to, and a denial of, everything that I had been taught to believe from the moment I was old enough to think."

Levi rose to his feet again and placed his empty cup on the silver salver. "Of course," he said, looking down on Tullius, "as the answers began to materialize, I quickly came to appreciate an amazing truth: I had been searching blindly, in dusty, shadowy corners and secret places, when the answers were all in the open, plainly visible to any man who knew what to look for."

"Nonsense." The Roman's voice *was* a whisper now. "Nothing is in the open."

"Really?" Levi stood up again and moved away from the table, towards the window. "Nothing is in the open in the normal sense, and yet in quite another sense, it is. But the truth is transparently concealed behind one fact that hides it from men's eyes."

The soldiers who had paraded on the other side of the street were gone. The street was deserted now except for a few straggling pedestrians, and the dust had settled into a thick, warm blanket over the cobblestones. Levi turned, leaning his back against the sill of the window, seeing his shadow hard and black across a different stretch of flooring, the shape of his head askew against the far wall. He had lost track of time.

Tullius cleared his throat. "And what is that? That fact?"

Levi looked down and adjusted the drape of his long overgarment, then spoke from where he was, knowing that Tullius, no matter how hard he squinted, could not see his face against the glare of the light behind him.

"The fact is that the truth is so evident, and so monstrous, that ordinary men cannot bring themselves to believe the evidence that is in front of them. Your family name is Tullius, but you are directly related, by blood, to the Seneca clan, the richest on earth. They finance all of Rome! Everything! Nothing of note that happens in the Roman world, or beyond it in the barbarian lands, happens without the financial involvement, at some level, of the Seneca clan. That defies belief—and yet it is true, from all that I have found, even with the small resources I possess. And the clan's wealth came to them from down the centuries, didn't it? It came out of Athens and Troy, and out of Macedon, and Nineveh, and Tyre, accumulated by ancestors stretching back to the beginnings of time. Rome may rule the world in the eyes of ordinary men, but your clan rules Rome! And when Rome is finished, as Greece was, and Macedon, and Carthage, your clan will survive, with all its wealth, located somewhere else. Am I not right?"

"You were correct to wonder. I should have you incarcerated as a madman."

"Too late, Caius Tullius. I know now what I know."

"So to whom do you intend to tell this fantastic tale?"

Levi returned to his chair. "To all who would believe me. And I already have. They were few. Most men, were they to hear my views, would think me mad."

"And the few who did not? What do these intend to do?"

"What *can* they do? They will live by the rules set up by you—live within the system. But they are aware, and knowledge is power."

"Hmm! Power again."

"Of course."

"So, you would pit your power against this clan's?"

"Caius Tullius! That would be folly. We will use our understanding to coexist within the system."

"If you are permitted to live . . . possessing such knowledge, I mean, and assuming it to be accurate."

"Now you are being provocative." Solomon Levi smiled. "In any case, I will not die before I make my point, which you were at such pains to wrest from me. Certainly, you can have me killed. You have that power. But consider this: I could kill you now, before the help you might summon could arrive. I would die, but you would, too. And what end would be served? No . . ." Unhurriedly now, Levi stood and moved to refill his empty wine cup, then replenished Tullius's, who made no move to pick it up.

"The power of life and death is not true power, Caius Tullius. Personal knowledge is unconquerable, yet there is nothing personal in your clan's power, which is why it is powerless against people like me. My life's true work is already done. I have passed on my knowledge. I have long since spread my ideas, and that is what will blunt your clan's power, someday, if anything can, in the eyes of free men."

"There are no free men." Tullius's voice was hushed.

"Ah, but there are. You have not been listening as closely as you ought. Freedom—true freedom—exists in the mind of the thinking man, and only there, and that is one place power like yours cannot penetrate. Can you not see that? Men who are thus free enjoy the freedom to ignore your power and to despise you, to defy you, and to expose you for what you are, if they so wish."

He broke off, then continued. "You disappointed me, Caius Tullius. I told you Ichabod was the second most powerful man in our village, and I expected you to ask me who the *most* powerful man was." He paused again, until he judged that Tullius would not rise to his bait. "My father was the most powerful man in our community. He was a builder, like me. A master builder, trained in the ancient crafts of the architects who built the great Temple on the plain behind us, erected by King Solomon, my namesake. And that is why you will not have me killed or thrown into a dungeon—because you know that people like you need people like me. You live in palaces, but you can't build them, not with all the slaves in the world, because our lore, the craft of the master builders, is secret, held in the mind, and painstakingly acquired throughout a lifetime of learning and doing. You may extract the theory, by torture or by guile, but you can never extort the ability to design, or to gauge at a glance what is structurally correct and what is not. Your power requires the builders, the architects, the engineers, the contractors, the free men, in order to portray itself. In all things there is balance. Your great trading houses must be built—your temples to trade and commerce, to Baal, to wealth, wherein you wield your power—but you would be roofless without our skills, our tools, and our knowledge.

"Look closely at King Solomon's Temple next time you pass by it. It was built by men like me."

Tullius slammed his open palm down on the tabletop. "But it was paid for by men like me! Where do you think Solomon acquired the wealth to build it? From us! He had the dream of appeasing his god, but we, and only we, had the wealth to make his dream a reality. Just as we have the wealth to tear it down tomorrow should it suit our purpose to wipe it from the earth. The Great Temple of Solomon the Wise!" His voice quivered with anger.

"You do," Solomon Levi agreed calmly. "But it does not alter the balance I spoke of. Your wealth can never wipe out the *memory* of the Temple, the fact that it once stood, that it was built. Nor can it purchase the skills and abilities to rebuild it—you will still need men like me, free, knowledgeable, and of good will. In that endeavour, Master Tullius, your mighty clan is not merely powerless. It is useless. You may have me killed now, but all your power would be useless in any attempt you might make to convince me to permit you to rule my thoughts, or to allow you to exist without condemning you . . . or *understanding* you! My life is nothing, but my skills, my abilities, and my *knowledge* already reside in the minds and in the hearts of those who will take my place. And not simply tomorrow, Caius Tullius, but down through the years and the centuries."

He rose to his feet. "And now I will leave you. I have an enterprise to conclude, premises to close down, and a family to care for. No doubt you have letters to write, to your own family. I wish you well at their hands."

Solomon Levi turned and left the room, a tall, broad old man with long, grey hair and a youthful, confident step. He made no attempt to close the door behind him, knowing that the servant posted there would do that without thinking, and he did not even glance again towards the window where, in his curule chair, the Roman Caius Tullius sat slack-jawed, a handsome, far younger man, bowed with the weight of his power, the lines in his cheeks now pronounced and deep-graven as he slumped on bent arms across the table's polished top, his eyes staring straight ahead into some unknown depth.

After a long time, without looking, the banker groped for his cup of wine and his fingers displaced the symmetry of the pyramidal pile of tightly rolled parchments, sending them tumbling, some of them to the mosaic floor. Tullius ignored them, staring into some emptiness ahead of him. His hand remained flat on the tabletop, his fingers within inches of the cup he had been seeking. The cry of a human voice filtered into the room from outside and died away. The sunbeam faded gradually, free of dust.

A Good Walk Spoiled

The story that follows deals with a time, and a way of life, that no longer exists: a time when the restricted world I lived in was ruled by bad-tempered, humourless adult males. Nowadays, as an adult myself, I can see that in most instances, it really wasn't the fault of the individual men, because they themselves had been reared in a dour, humourless, and all too often hypocritical Calvinist society that left them hidebound by harsh and crippling expectations that were, almost by definition, incapable of being met. Those unfortunate Scots males, most of them Presbyterian and reared between the two world wars, had to live according to stifling behavioural codes of sixteenth-century puritanism that constrained the men themselves just as much as—and sometimes even worse than—they affected the other people, men and women, boys and girls, who were bullied and browbeaten by them.

As a healthy pre-teenaged boy, it was an integral part of my duties, and of my nature, to confound any limitations that unsmiling grown-ups tried to impose on me. My friends and I had absolutely no idea of where, when, or how adulthood began, but we had no desire to experience it, and we refused to kowtow to it. Adults were the enemy: the Great Unknown. It didn't matter to us who they were in their own eyes—crabby old men, dirty old men, scruffy old men, and disapproving old men, they all appeared to us to exist solely to interfere with our enjoyment of life, and so we took great pleasure in hoodwinking them, sidestepping their disapproval and getting on with things we really needed to do.

No one ever told us that we were learning behaviour patterns of our own that would accompany us through life. But there are times today when I realize just how blessed my friends and I were to live at that time.

Kids today have gadgets, computers, and smart phones; we had long summer evenings of running wild through woodlands that had never welcomed our working-class families or heard our unabashed laughter before, lands that had been carefully tended for hundreds of years and were full of game birds—pheasant, partridge, and grouse. We were free, in our boyhood, to walk or run along the rich, rhododendron-bordered bridle paths that lined the banks of rivers teeming with brown and speckled trout, our imaginations staggering with the excesses of our surroundings. And yet despite the half century of distance between my boyhood environment and the technological universe that kids inhabit today, not too many of the eternal verities have changed, just as the essential nature of adolescence itself hasn't changed since organized societies began: the Adolescent Creed exhorts each new generation to mature as no one ever has before. "Come to your own terms with life," it says. "Don't let anyone else tell you how to live or think. And above all, pay no attention to old folk, for they know nothing about what we're discovering."

The next three stories, then, describe events that occurred to a group of three boys in a part of central Scotland on a single day in the early 1950s. Two of those boys are now dead, but I, the sole remaining participant, remember these incidents with stark clarity, perhaps because I was the leader of the pack in those days. Until recently, though, I had always remembered that day as an exciting, fun-filled one, the hands-down pinnacle of that year's summer holidays and the embodiment of the answer to the perennial challenge of every new school year: the inevitable essay on the topic, "How I spent my summer holidays."

It was only very recently that the real truth about that long-ago day dawned on me, when something jogged my memory and set me thinking of my two old school chums and the times we had together before we were forced to grow up. I realized that these incidents hadn't happened quite as precisely as I recalled them, on one single, halcyon day. But there is an undeniable emotional truth to that conceit, and so that is how I've chosen to present them here, with fictitious names to protect the unsuspecting.

I

In the middle of the last century, before the growth of mass tourism, the few visiting tourists were often surprised to find sheep grazing on the fairways of rural Scottish golf courses, but it was common until quite recently. The grazing animals kept the grass short in times of petrol rationing, and golfers accepted the piles of dung they left as an inexpensive, natural means of ensuring the continuing good condition of the fairways. Surprisingly few people ever actually hit a sheep with a ball. The eye of the practised golfer makes its allowances subconsciously and avoids sending the ball towards anything that constitutes a blatant hazard. On the few occasions when a badly hit ball does strike a sheep, usually the only damage done is to the golfer's score and temper, since the sting of any impact tends to be absorbed by the animal's thick fleece. Barry Taylor's shot, then, was simply unlucky, but its effect was devastating.

Barry, Andy McNeil, and Greg Pearson had been out on the course at Bellside as soon as it opened that day, on a perfect late-August Saturday morning more than halfway through the summer holidays. Their fourth player had been a no-show, and so they had been taking great care to draw as little attention to themselves as possible, because threesomes were discouraged on Scots golf courses in the 1950s: foursomes were the norm, pairs were acceptable, and single walkers were considered harmless, but threesomes, for some obscure reason, were perceived as being cumbersome, unpredictable, and verging upon outright illegality. Old Toby Finch, the head greenskeeper, offered no quarter to any boys who attracted his attention, but he was merciless to threesomes comprising boys. This particular trio had been surprised by how few people were out on the course on such a glorious morning, by the shortness of the time they had had to wait, and most of all by the hard-to-believe knowledge that Finch had failed to notice there were only three of them that day. The wait by the tee box had been nerve-wracking, but once they were off and away, Barry had won the first hole with a par and the second and third with bogeys, halving the fourth hole at bogey with Andy and feeling extremely pleased with himself. And then his drive from the fifth found a sheep in the middle distance and hit it unerringly, directly behind the ear, and the animal went down as though it had been shot, while its neighbours scattered. The three boys watched in awed silence as the animal staggered unsteadily back to its feet, then fell sideways again and rolled onto its back, its feet sticking straight up into the air.

"Jesus Christ," whispered Andy McNeil. "You killed it!"

Neither of the other boys spoke, as all three of them stared in horror at the motionless animal. Then Barry dropped his golf bag and took off running towards the sheep, closely followed by his friends, until they threw themselves to their knees beside the motionless beast.

"How can we check if it's still alive?" Andy was breathing more heavily than the others; he had carried his golf bag with him.

"Take its pulse," Greg Pearson suggested.

"Come on, Greg, this is serious!" There was the beginning of panic in Barry Taylor's voice. "What are we going to do?"

"Jesus Christ," said Andy again. "It's stone dead."

Barry turned on him. "Is that all you can say, for Christ's sake? We know it's dead. The question is what the hell are we going to do about it?"

"What d'ye mean, we?" Andy shot back. "You were the one that killed it. What are *you* going to do about it?"

Barry felt his temper flaring. "Andy, if you don't shut your stupid head, I'll lay you out here beside it."

"Aye," added Greg. "And if he can't manage it on his own, I'll help him!"

It was no time for bickering. The sheep was dead and the least that was going to happen was that someone was going to have to pay for it, since sheep were valuable animals, although none of the boys could have begun to guess what one was worth. It stood to reason, though, that somebody, undoubtedly some frowning man of power and prestige, was going to have to get paid. Barry could feel his stomach twisting and he had visions of having to forfeit all his pocket money for the next ten years.

Greg wrinkled his nose. "Whew! It doesn't half stink!"

"It's rottin' already," Andy said.

Barry ignored the rancid, slightly sweet smell. He was looking at a clump of bushes, scrubby and thick, in the long rough about twenty yards from where the boys were standing. "Quick," he said. "Nobody's seen us yet. We might be able to get away with it. We'll drag it over behind those bushes. If anyone finds it, they won't know who killed it." His voice was filled with authority now. "Greg, take the hind legs," he continued. "I'll take the front. Andy, you go back up the fairway and keep an eye out for anybody coming. If there's anybody up there, keep them out of sight until we've finished."

"How will I do that?" Andy's voice sounded plaintive.

"Do what?"

"Keep them out of the way. If there's anyone coming."

"Talk to them, you daft bastard, what d'you think?"

"What'll I talk about?"

"Jesus Christ! Now he wants to get shy! Ask them what the jail sentence is for being an accomplice to cattle rustlers! How the hell do I know what you're supposed to say? Just open your mouth and let your belly rumble. You're good at that at any other time."

Andy stood, his face expressionless, until Barry exploded. "For God's sake, Andy! Will you get going before somebody catches us standing here like the Three Stooges? Whistle if you see anybody comin', okay? One whistle if they're not too close, two whistles if they're closer, and three if they're very close. Okay?"

Andy nodded, still looking dazed.

Barry bent to take hold of the sheep's legs. "Okay, Greg, pull like a bastard."

Andy took off then, running back up the fairway towards the tee, and Barry and Greg began to struggle with the dead weight of the sheep. They had managed to get it all the way across the fairway, into the edge of the long rough, before Andy's whistle came. They stopped in mid-pull. He whistled again. Close, but not too close. They glanced at each other in relief and had just started to pull again when the third whistle sounded. Too damn close! They were about five yards from the bushes.

"Quick," Barry panted. "One more hard pull!" They heaved together with all their strength and the carcass of the sheep tobogganed over the long grass towards the bushes just as Andy began to sound a long series of whistles like a skylark. The two boys had time only to drag the sheep beneath the hanging branches of the bushes at the rear edge of the clump and leave it there, with the slender bulk of the bush between the carcass and the tee box. After that, all they could do was pray that it wouldn't be discovered until they were long departed.

They raced back to the fairway, trying to look innocent, and snatched up burdock leaves from the rough and tried to rub the stench of sheep from their hands. Andy was on the tee box with their golf bags lying close to him, and they could see the heads of two men approaching him over the top of the hillock behind it. Both boys stuffed their hands in their pockets, but Barry's heart sank as he recognized the older of the two men now striding towards them. It was Sandy Baxter, the bad-tempered wealthy old man who lived in the huge house between Barry's home and Greg's. Baxter had no love for either boy, and he had once called the police just because he saw Barry running along the top of his garden wall, taking the shortcut to Greg's house.

"What the hell are you young buggers doin' out here on a Saturday? It's no' what it's supposed to be, I'll wager on that! If you're out here at all you're supposed to be playin' at the golf, no' skylarkin' about like damned Indians and annoyin' God-fearin' decent folk that come out for a quiet game to get away from the likes o' you!"

"Hello, Mr. Baxter," Barry said. The other two boys flushed.

"Don't 'hello' me! Just stand away from the box and let us play through. If you canna play well enough or fast enough to stay in front, then you'll be good enough to stay behind us. *Well* behind us! We ha'e nae need to be bothered wi' the likes of you breathin' down our necks and upsettin' our game. Bloody young hooligans . . ."

Baxter's companion, a much younger man, winked at the boys as they hastily removed their golf bags from the tee and stood well out of the old man's line of sight.

Baxter teed up his ball and prepared to address it, muttering under his breath. No one else spoke, and Baxter took his time, waggling his club head behind the ball and settling himself comfortably for his swing. But his backswing was much too fast, and his stroke no better than a hacking slash. The head of the club whipped the tee cleanly from underneath the ball, which went two feet up in the air and landed in the same spot where the tee had been.

The old man's reflexes were superb, though. The ball had hardly even reached the top of its hop when he turned to his companion, saying, "Losh, Lord, man oh man, what am I thinking of? You won the last hole, did you not, Robert? It's no' my turn at all! I beg your pardon, son, the honour's still yours." He stepped back magnanimously to allow his partner the "first" shot.

Robert inclined his head politely and stepped forward to tee up his ball, only the slightest hint of a smile on his face. "Thank you," he said, and all three boys knew that he must be aching to point out that old Baxter's next shot would be two off the tee. The hole was a 370-yard par four with a downhill dogleg to the left and a small green almost completely hidden by trees and high-sided bunkers.

Barry was surprised to see that Robert, whoever he was, was holding a two-iron, but the tall young man unleashed a slow, clean, lazy-looking swing that hammered his ball a good two hundred yards out with a gentle, drifting hook that took it beautifully around the dogleg and kept it running like a hare long after it had hit.

"Lovely shot, mister," Greg Pearson said. "Well away!" The other boys echoed him.

Robert winked at them. "Thanks, lads."

Old man Baxter looked fit to be tied. "Aye," he mumbled. "No' bad, no' bad." He stepped forward again and teed up his ball, and then he seemed to take forever to line up his shot. When he swung this time, he hit a beauty. His ball took off as though it would fly forever, and all three boys followed it with their eyes in grudging admiration. Then, right at the top of its flight, Baxter's ball began to fade to the right, slicing more and more rapidly, and with a sense of poetic justice, Barry Taylor knew exactly where it was going.

Sure enough, it landed right in the first bush in the long rough to the right of the fairway. Exactly where they had left the dead sheep.

Nobody uttered a sound during the entire flight of the ball, not even old Baxter, who stood as though carved from stone, his body twisted and his arms frozen at the top of his follow-through. He marked where the ball landed and then relaxed.

None of the boys dared look at the others, each of them horribly certain that the jig was up. The old man's ball must be within arm's reach of the dead sheep. They were all convinced that old Baxter would find the dead animal, put two and two together, and come up with three . . . them!

"I'll come with you," Robert said, "and help you look for it."

"Thank ye, Robert, but that will no' be necessary. I saw fine where it landed, and I'll have nae trouble findin' it, though it might gi'e me a wee bit o' bother chippin' it back out onto the fairway. Away ye go and see to your own shot."

The boys watched numbly as the two men left the tee and walked off together down the fairway, the older man pulling his wheeled cart behind him. When they reached the point at which their paths separated, Robert to the left and old Baxter towards the dead sheep, the old man suddenly turned back and brandished his niblick at the three boys like a battle-axe as he shouted at the top of his voice, "Ye'll mind, now, what I said, and just haud yourselves in patience till we're away out in front. I dinna want any o' your damn balls fleein' about my ears!" His warning delivered, he strode away.

"Jesus Christ," said Andy McNeil. "Now we're really for it! They'll put us in jail. I knew fine we should have reported it."

Barry Taylor gave him a baleful scowl.

"What're you lookin' at me like that for?" Andy said. "It was an accident, wasn't it. You didn't *aim* at the fuckin' sheep, did you. It wasna done wi' malice aforethought, was it. The stupid thing just got in the way o' the ball." He glared from one to the other of his silent friends. "It was an accident. A sheer accident. We could've reported it and been fine."

Old Baxter was approaching the point of no return.

"But oh no!" Andy pressed on. "We couldn't do that! Not us! Mr. Big Al Ca-fuckin'-pone Taylor has to be smart and hide the evidence. 'Nobody'll know,' he says. 'How's anybody gonnae know?' An' now the three o' us are gonnae get arrested."

Barry grasped Andy by the jacket and tried to wrestle him to the ground to shut him up. But Greg Pearson had been watching the old man all the time, and now he threw himself on his two friends.

"Lookit," he cried, shaking both of them. "Look at this!"

They looked.

Baxter was stabbing around the base of the bush, looking for his ball, and the sheep, miraculously alive, was heading towards him from the rear, out of the old man's sight. All three boys cheered at seeing the animal alive, and old Baxter, hearing them and thinking they were jeering him, shook his club angrily at them.

"It's alive! Jesus Christ, it's alive!" Andy was jumping up and down, yelling at the top of his voice. "It must've just been knocked out!"

Greg Pearson sobered all of them by saying, "Aye, it's alive, all right, but look at the way it's walking."

The wretched animal looked as though it was drunk. It was staggering from side to side, teetering and tottering, unable to find its balance. Suddenly it went down on its knees, and the boys fell silent in mid-cheer. But it lurched back to its feet and began walking again, and still the old man had not noticed it. He had found his ball and was hacking wildly at the long grass and fibrous, wiry thistles that could hamper his next swing.

The boys watched silently as Baxter straightened, focused his concentration, and delivered his stroke. By that time, though, the sheep was only a few feet away from him. The old man must have caught sight of it just as he reached the top of his backswing, for he straightened up violently in mid-stroke, flubbed the shot badly, and sent his ball careering off into deep rough: dense gorse and long, coarse grass. The boys heard a scream of rage as he took another swing, this time over his head, at the unfortunate sheep, which promptly collapsed at his feet.

By the time they reached him, out of breath from the effort of running with their golf bags, Mr. Baxter had lost any thought of being rude. In response to their questions about what had happened, he merely shook his head in bewilderment and muttered that he didn't know. The damned thing had frightened the life out of him, he said, and made him miss his stroke, after which he had taken a swipe at it and it had fallen down. He could hardly believe it, he mumbled, because he didn't think he had swung that hard. His voice tailed away.

Andy was on his knees by the sheep. He pulled open one of its eyes the way he had seen such things done in films. "You should have missed this shot, too, Mr. Baxter," he said. "It's dead."

This time there was absolutely no doubt about it. The sheep was irrefutably dead.

The man called Robert had been on his way back to help old Baxter when he saw the boys running, and now he came striding up, asking what was going on, and again it was Andy who got the first words out.

"Mr. Baxter killed a sheep. It made him miss his shot, so he clouted it wi' a club and killed it stone dead."

Robert's eyebrows rose about an inch. "Is that right? Did you?"

Baxter's face was ashy and he looked as though he might be sick any second. Barry felt desperately sorry for the man now, in spite of all the times in the past that Baxter had made his life miserable. The death-dealing club had fallen from his hands and now lay at his feet. Barry moved to pick it up.

"Mr. Baxter, for God's sake!" Robert's voice was urgent. "What happened?"

"I . . . I dinna ken, just rightly." The old man's voice was very low. "I was just about to play my shot when I saw this damned animal damn near runnin' intae me. It was so close it scared me, ye ken, and my damn ba' took a flee right off the toe o' my club intae the gorse yonder. I was so mad, I took a skelp at the sheep wi' my club. It didna even try to jouk—it just stood there, and then it fell doon. The laddies saw it. Aye, the laddies was watchin'. They saw it."

The younger man looked at each of the three boys in turn. "Is that what you saw?"

All three nodded.

Robert went down on one knee beside the sheep and placed his hand on its neck, his thumb beneath the jawbone, and then he, too, lifted the eyelid. The eye was already glazed. "Dead as mutton," he said. He looked up at Baxter. "Where did you hit it?"

"I . . . I'm no' sure. I think I caught it o'er the shoulder. The left one."

Robert ran his hand deftly from the animal's left shoulder up to its ear, where he stopped. "Well," he said, "there's a lump here the size of a goose egg, right on the bone behind the ear. No wonder you killed it. If it had been an elephant you'd still have killed it. You must have given it one hell of a clout."

"But I didna." The old man's voice was almost quavering. "I didna hit it that hard, Robert, I couldna. I'm no' that strong."

Robert smiled a little half smile. "Is that a fact? You're as strong as a bull, Hector. I've been your doctor now for seven years, so I know. I told you that temper of yours would get you into trouble one day." He shook his head. "You know, before I married your daughter, I used to worry in case she turned out to have your personality instead of her mother's." He stood up and placed his hand on the old man's shoulder. "Well, come on, then. We'd better go and report this. Whose sheep are these, anyway?"

It was Greg Pearson who answered him. "Gillespie's."

"Which Gillespie?" There were three Gillespie brothers, all farming contiguous plots of land.

"Angus."

"Aye, well, we'd better go and have a talk with him, Father Baxter . . ." Robert's voice faded away as he considered something, and then he went on. "I suppose we could finish our game first. It wouldn't do much harm. But then, I suspect your heart wouldn't be in it, would it? I know mine wouldn't."

"Will Mr. Baxter have to go to jail?"

Robert looked in surprise at Greg and laughed aloud.

"Good Lord, no! Whatever gave you that idea?" In spite of his laughter, or perhaps because of it, he slowly became aware of the concern on the faces of all three boys. "Look, lads," he said, quietly and seriously. "Every farmer who grazes his sheep on a golf course accepts the risk of losing the occasional animal to a hard-hit ball, because the chances of it actually happening must be a million to one. But if it does happen, there's nothing for the farmer to do but complain to the club executive, and he'll get short shrift there, since he's been benefiting from free grazing privileges." He looked at each of the boys, weighing his next words. "This is simply an extension of that circumstance, except that Mr. Baxter hit the sheep with his club, not with his ball. Not much difference, though. The sheep's still dead. Mr. Baxter, however, will accept the responsibility and pay Angus Gillespie a fair price for the dead animal. Isn't that so, Mr. Baxter?"

The old man had been standing listening, a vacant expression on his face. Now he nodded and made a sound in his throat that everyone accepted as agreement.

Robert continued to eye the boys. "Is that all right with you three?"

Surprised that they should even be consulted, the boys nodded eagerly.

The younger man thanked them gravely, apologized for having interrupted their game, and then ensured their silence by borrowing his father-in-law's wallet and bestowing a crisp new one-pound note—an unheard-of fortune—upon each of them, before leading the old man away towards the clubhouse.

The boys looked at each other and then at the pound notes they held in their hands. None of them had ever actually owned a pound note before. Now they were content for a few moments simply to look at their riches and dream.

It was Greg who broke the silence. "Hey, look," he said. "We've been played through."

They had, too. One foursome was already pitching onto the green at the bottom of the hill, and another foursome was approaching a clean quartet of tee shots that lay, all white and shiny, in the middle of the fairway opposite where the boys still stood in the long rough.

The boys decided they had had enough golf for that day, anyway, and set out for home. They crossed the golf course diagonally in front of the clubhouse, heading for the rhododendron bushes that marked the rim of the river gorge that meandered cross-country to pass within half a mile of their homes. It was a four-mile walk to where they lived, but they were used to it and had proved many times that by walking that route, they could get home as quickly as they could by taking the main road through town and waiting for the bus.

"Jeez," Andy McNeil wondered aloud, "what d'ye do wi' a whole pound?"

II

The voices were far away, but the first sound of them was enough to cause the flock of crows in the clearing to whirl up and away, squawking with alarm, in search of safety among the high branches that surrounded the open glade on three sides. Once there, safely settled and fortified with the security of height, they faced the approaching sounds. The two young people who came along the pathway on the hillside above, oblivious to everything except their love for each other, would never have seen them had the birds' movements not caught the eye of the boy as they passed by at eye level. He had one arm around the girl, who walked close against him, her head resting on his shoulder so that he could smell the freshness of her hair beneath his cheek.

"Hey," he whispered. "Don't look now, but we're being watched."

The girl started away from him with a guilty leap, looking around her in fright. "What? Who's there? Where?" Her voice was almost comical but her anxiety was very real, and the young man reached for her again and pulled her close.

"Hey, hey! It's all right, I was only kidding, Annie, I'm sorry. There's some crows watching us, that's all." He supported her chin with one hand and turned her head to follow as he aimed his finger at their silent, wary audience. "Look, in the trees there. See?" She looked, nervously, and then turned her face into the hollow of his shoulder, and he gentled the back of her head in his hand. "I'm sorry, Annie. Jeez, I didn't mean to scare you."

Her voice came to him muffled by the material of his jacket. "You frightened the life out of me. I thought some dirty old man was spying on us." Slowly she withdrew her head and looked back at the crows. "They *are* watching us, aren't they?"

He laughed. "Sure they are. They're lookin' at you. I would be, too, if I was up there wi' them. There's nothin' better to look at round this place. You know what they say, 'A cat can look at a king.' I suppose that means a crow can look at a beautiful lassie. But they really are ugly buggers, aren't they?" The crows continued to stare, stark and disapproving and managing to look aggressive without even moving.

Annie shuddered. "I hate those things."

"Hate them?" There was humour and surprise in the boy's voice. "What for? They're just birds."

"No! They're *not* just birds. They're filthy things. Scavengers. My grandpa used to hate them, too. He used to shoot them. He said they used to eat the dead men in the trenches in the First World War. He used to call them 'hoodies.'"

"Aye, but they're not. 'Hoodies' are hooded crows. Their grey feathers look like a hood and sometimes like a cape, too, but their wings are black and they're very different from carrion crows. The carrion crows are the worst when it comes to scavenging, though—even their name tells you that—and they're all dead black. But all crows are man-eaters if they find a corpse. Those things watching us now, though, they're rooks—they're scavengers, too, but rooks is their real name and they're a completely different bird. They've got grey feathers round their heads too, though, so that makes them look like hoodies and gets them a bad name."

"Carrion eaters are disgusting things."

"Carrion eaters?" The boy grinned. "Carrion?"

"Aye, dead meat."

"I know what it is, I just didn't expect you to."

Annie's eyes flashed. "And why not? D'you think I'm styoopit?"

"No, I don't, and that was a stupid thing to say, I'm sorry. But we eat dead meat too, Annie."

"Not carrion!"

"Sure we do! Dead meat."

"Och! You're ridiculous, Eamonn McShane! Carrion, for your information, is dead meat that's been left to rot where it fell, guts and all. There's a big difference between that and meat that's been slaughtered and butchered and cleaned for human consumption."

"Consumption? The fellow who used to live next door to us has consumption. He's in a sanatorium now, but they think he'll probably get better. Is that right, you can get consumption from eating butcher meat? I thought it was from drinking unpasteurized milk."

Annie swung a slap at his ear, laughing in exasperation. He ducked, and as he did so the watching birds stirred nervously, one of them seeming to rise on tiptoe, its wings spread, poised to take off. Eamonn straightened up slowly, watching it, and the bird settled down again.

The girl saw the expression in his eyes and her voice held a hint of concern when she asked, "What's the matter?"

Eamonn nodded towards the watching birds. "I was just thinking that you're right. They're no' very nice, are they? Kinda menacing . . . Scary. Have you ever read 'The Twa Corbies'?"

She frowned slightly. "No. Who wrote it?"

"Nobody. It's ancient, medieval. One of the old ballads. Do they not teach you anything at that school you go to?"

"Well certainly not about poems that write themselves! I never heard anything so daft. You mean it's anonymous."

"Aye, that's what I said . . . anomalous."

"Eamonn McShane, that's another word altogether and you know it. Anyway, what're corbies?"

"Crows. That's the old Scotch word for them. It's a poem—a song, really—about two crows that find a dead knight behind a wall. Nobody's come looking for him, no one cares about burying him, and the crows talk about what happened to him, about how his hound's run off hunting, his hawk's gone back to the wild, and his wife's already remarried, leaving him as food for the crows. Finally one says to the other, 'You'll sit on his white breastbone, and I'll pick out his sweet blue een, an' wi' a lock of his golden hair we'll thatch our nest when it grows bare.'"

The girl shuddered again in the warm sunlight and glanced back up at the birds on their branches. "That's disgusting, but I can believe it. There's not much separating civilization from savagery . . . Let's go, Eamonn, I don't like it here."

"Aye, okay, but watch this!" He stooped quickly and pretended to snatch up a stone from the pathway, cocking his arm to throw as he rose, and the birds flung themselves into the air, swooping and soaring in all directions, their raucous cries shockingly loud in the stillness. "See that? Talk about reflexes! Crows ar'na daft. Point a gun or a stick, pick up a stone, and they're away before you can aim, even when you think they're no' watching you. And when you do something like that, and the birds squawk in triple caws, that's a sure sign that they're corbies. Carrion crows, the real McCoy." He smiled at her. "Come on, then, let's keep going. It's a grand day for a walk, now that the rain's stopped." Annie came back into the closeness of his arm and they walked on, oblivious of all but themselves.

As the young couple turned to go, the crows returned, one by one, to perch in the branches, their heads moving jerkily from one side to the other as they watched the intruders leave, and below in the clearing the day's normal noises began to reassert themselves. Fat bumblebees buzzed lazily among the rioting rhododendron blossoms, and gnats and other winged insects busied themselves among the willow weed and foxgloves on the hillside. And in the marshy, waterlogged sedge surrounding the bog hole at the middle of the clearing, a weathered, discoloured human thigh bone thrust upward among the reeds.

***

The boys had decided to walk home from the golf course along the riverbank and through the old estate, carrying their clubs. They were in no hurry, and they walked through a glorious morning, in a silence broken only by birdsong and the chuckling gurgle of the river in its gorge below. The sound of their footsteps, even had they not been trying to walk like forest-wise Indians, would have been drowned by a years-thick carpet of dead leaves and pine needles. Everything else around them, except the bark of the tree boles, was bright, lush green. Great clumps of bracken fern grew in profusion alongside their path, and there were rhododendrons everywhere. The trunks of the trees were coated with thick, dank moss, and the stillness of the woods seemed tangible.

Their path led them past the tumbled, overgrown ruins of an old grey sandstone castle, the only part of it left standing being the outer walls of the high, almost windowless keep with the stepped gables that defined it as Scottish. Beyond that, the path, which had been covered at some time during the previous fifty to a hundred years with rust-red cinder clinker, swept steeply down towards the river in a series of swooping, ten- to fifteen-yard drops punctuated by man-made steps. At the bottom, mere yards above where the currents brawled among large boulders, the boys emerged onto a wide, hard-packed path that followed the bank of the river.

As they went down the last descending stretch, though, they sensed and heard movement below and ahead of them. Andy McNeil was the first to notice, and he stopped dead in his tracks, waving a stiff-armed warning to his friends behind him, who froze in place, wary and silent. They had done nothing wrong, but they were in "Tiger Country," and they needed no lessons in being cautious.

The lands surrounding them, a massive tract of contiguous estates that had originally covered fifty to sixty square miles, had been owned for centuries by the regional aristocracy that the local peasantry called, not always fondly or subserviently, the gentry. There had never been any need of walls or gates there, since the owner-occupiers of the enclave were all known to one another and wandered freely afoot and on horseback from manor to manor, secure in their privileged privacy. The lower-class village peasantry from beyond their ornate iron gates were unequivocally excluded, save only for the staff required to keep the manor houses running and the kitchens functioning, the gardeners who tended the exteriors, and the small army of ground workers and gamekeepers who kept the inventory of game—deer, foxes, hares, pheasant, grouse, partridges, and fishing stocks of trout and bream—in plentiful supply.

The onset of the First World War had marked the beginning of the end of that era. The old established order began to change rapidly with the ravaging scourge of wartime casualties—an entire generation of young leaders simply vanished in the Flanders mud—

and with the postwar establishment of the earth-shaking age of socialism. The wealth that had sustained the old order for several centuries migrated invisibly into new endeavours and new enterprise. And the remnants of the formerly aristocratic families were increasingly reduced to insignificance, weakened to impotence by war and natural attrition, and impoverished by rapidly escalating costs that devoured their petty individual family "riches" and introduced them willy-nilly to the novel ideas of penury and ultimate obliteration during the quarter-century that followed the armistice of 1918. Their riches, their societal pretensions, and their entire upper-class world were all destroyed by unsustainable, socialist-driven property taxes and the new and intolerable death duties that were levied by hungry, increasingly socialist governments on the estates of everyone rich enough to die while still owning an estate.

And so, by the 1950s, the old estates, monuments to the aristocratic excesses of eighteenth- and nineteenth-century society, had all fallen into disuse, disrepair, and ever-increasing bankruptcies. The last of them in that area of the country had vanished completely by the end of the Second World War, and their erstwhile leisure properties, close to sixty square miles of prime land in Lanarkshire alone, had been broken up and seized, mostly in forfeitures for unpaid taxes, by the governments of the surrounding municipalities.

Plans were in hand to subdivide the former estates for development, but government moves notoriously slowly and those abandoned lands were left open for the time being, a fantastical, otherworldly paradise for adventurous young boys, and as common land for anyone else who cared to go there. And that, unfortunately, included many people whose activities might be construed elsewhere as lawless, or at least as being inconsiderate of the public good. Plainly speaking, there was always a risk, no matter who you were or where you were within the maze of pathways, of encountering people or things about which you might have wanted to remain ignorant. Which was why some wag had named the place Tiger Country.

And so, alerted and on guard, the three boys pulled off into the waist-high growth beside the path, where they crouched, tense but unseen, behind a dense screen of bracken ferns and a giant old tree stump. And there they remained, unmoving, as the besotted young lovers called Eamonn and Annie meandered slowly by, deep in soul-baring conversation. The three boys waited until the last sounds of the couple's quiet passage had disappeared, then returned to the path.

"Lucky bastard," growled Andy McNeil. He moved on down the hillside, followed by the others, towards the bridle path that edged the river. The boys ambled along in comfortable silence for another three or four hundred yards, until they took a familiar narrow track that led back towards the river that had curved away from them. It was an old game trail, really, little more than a worn rut, but it would follow the river's edge directly to the culvert beneath the main-road bridge, where they would emerge from the woods close to the edge of town and their homes on Fraser Street.

After a while, they crested the steep rise to where their trail became a five-foot-wide path again, its surface made of packed sand. They were familiar with the place and had their own little tradition there. Andy took an old golf ball from his bag, dropped it onto the path, and began to dribble it like a soccer ball. Concentrating on his footwork, and unconscious of the weight of the golf bag slung from his shoulder, he shuffled ahead, keeping the ball close between his feet until he turned and flicked it back to his friends. The three tapped it gently back and forth to one another a few times and then Andy lobbed a pass gently to Greg, who trapped it neatly beneath his foot, spun on his heel, and flicked the ball to Barry. It was slightly too far to the side, and although Barry hitched his bag up and went for the ball, he missed it. Chagrined, he followed it to where it ended up, tapped it lightly to where he wanted it, and then put his boot to it. It shot between Andy and Greg like a bullet, caromed off a tree, and disappeared down the steep bank towards the river.

Andy McNeil stood as though paralyzed, staring along the flight path of the vanished ball. "You daft bastard! What'd you do that for?"

Barry shrugged in what might have been an apology. "I didn't mean to. It just happened. Sorry."

"You're *sorry*? Jesus Christ!"

"Come on, Andy," Greg murmured. "It was only an old has-been tattie. It had a big smile in it."

"Smile? Smile, my arse! That was a Dunlop 65. You know what they cost?" Andy always hated to lose a ball, no matter the circumstance.

Barry began to unzip his golf bag. "So what? Here, I'll give you another one."

"Stick it up your arse, Taylor! I don't want a fuckinother one, I want *that* one. So you'd better get down there and start looking for it, or else."

"Or else what?" Barry was half bent over, looking up at Andy from his crouch. This, too, was a familiar routine.

"Or else you know what."

"No, I—" Barry stopped, suddenly deciding that this wasn't worth arguing over. He laid his bag carefully on the path and set off into the long grass on the steep bank, knowing that he didn't have a hope in hell of finding the ball but unwilling to prolong any unpleasantness for such a petty reason. Greg followed him, leaving Andy standing sulking on the pathway.

"You know we're never going to find it, don't you?"

Barry didn't even bother to answer; his eyes scanned the ground. He moved off to the right. Greg shook his head and went left, and found the ball moments later, lying right in front of him on a tiny patch of open ground.

"Hey, Barry!" he shouted with surprise. "I've got it."

"Never mind that," Barry called. "Come and see what I've found."

Greg slid across the steep slope, clutching at bushes and shrubs to keep his balance, and came to a stop. Barry was pointing to a bicycle, firmly anchored, upside down, in the topmost canopy of a high-climbing, hugely overgrown clump of wild bramble bushes. It was clean, brightly gleaming, new-looking.

"Jeez! That's . . . Jeez. Whose is it?"

"How the hell would I know? Hey, Andy! Come down here!"

"Did you find my ball?"

"Aye, but come and see this."

They heard the clatter of Andy's golf bag joining the others on the ground, and then came the sliding of his boots as he tobogganed wildly down the hillside towards them to throw his arms around a sapling and stop himself, staring wide-eyed at the bike.

"It's a bike."

"Get away!"

A look of perplexity came over Andy's face. As Greg and Barry had done before him, he looked all around as though expecting to see the owner close by. "Whose is it?" he asked. "An' what's it doin' up there down here?"

"It's down here," Greg explained patiently, "because we were up there on the path above it and it's up there 'cause we're on the side o' a hill and it's a long way down to the bottom, where we'll have to start if we want to reach it. What do you think, Barry?"

Barry Taylor shrugged. "Search me."

"'Sa nice bike . . ." Andy was staring up at it with slitted, covetous eyes. "It's even got a kickstand. That's fancy."

None of the three boys made any further move towards the bicycle until Greg said, "Somebody must've threw it in there."

"Threw it?" Andy said. "What d'you mean?"

"He's right," Barry said. "Look where it is. The grass isn't trampled between here and there, and the bramble stalks aren't smashed up, except on the very top where the bike is. Somebody threw it in there."

"Why would somebody throw a new bike away?" Greg asked.

"Stole it," Andy said unambiguously. "Somebody stole it and threw it in here to hide it till the hue and cry dies down."

"Okay," Barry said, using the American expression that would have earned him a thick ear from any of his schoolteachers. "What do we do now?"

"What d'you mean?"

"Well, are we going to leave it here for the thief to come back for it, or are we going to take it to the police station and tell them where we found it?"

The three boys looked at each other in silence for a few seconds and then, as one, they moved forward to retrieve the bike from the bushes.

It turned out to be far easier said than done. The bottom of the giant bramble clump was at least twenty feet below where they were standing on the steeply sloping hillside, and the bicycle was well and truly lodged more than ten feet up from the ground, upside down in the sunlit centre of a massive tangle of long, flexible branches armed with vicious, bloodthirsty thorns.

They reached the bottom of the clump and scanned the daunting tangle of briars facing them.

"Fuck this," Andy McNeil snarled. "You'd need a machete to get in there, like they use in the Tarzan pictures. Failin' that, we're gonnae need some Jeezusly big sticks."

He dug into his pocket and produced a big, heavy First World War British Army pocket knife, prising it open to display a blade worn almost to a sickle shape by constant sharpening. His grandfather had carried it throughout two world wars and had given it to him the previous year, warning him, unnecessarily, that it was wickedly sharp. Now, within minutes of opening it, he and Barry each had a long, heavy club-like stick made from a hazel sapling. Greg Pearson retrieved his rusty, trusty old niblick from his golf bag, and all three began to beat at the bushes between them and the prize that dangled over their heads.

Each of them fell several times on the slippery incline, damaging themselves—faces, legs, arms, and hands—and their clothing on the bramble thorns. They were determined, though, and after a struggle that lasted more than half an hour, accompanied by increasingly breathless curses that would have scandalized their mothers, they finally managed to dislodge the bicycle from its high perch, only to discover, immediately, that several spokes on each wheel had sprung loose and were sticking out wildly on either side. All three boys looked disgustedly at this evidence of vandalism. None of them owned a bicycle anywhere near as fine as this one, and the thought of anyone simply throwing such a beautiful machine away, and damaging it in so doing, was more than they could comprehend.

Barry Taylor dropped to one knee and began to twist the broken spokes around their neighbours, so there would be sufficient clearance for the wheels to turn unhampered. "We'd better take this right to the cop shop," he said, "so let's get moving, before the ignorant bastard that stole it comes back and catches us."

Ten minutes later, having awkwardly wrestled the bike all the way up the steep, slick slope, they collected their bags and looked around them carefully, making sure that no one was watching them from the surrounding bushes. And then they set out for the police station, feeling measurably more confident.

They were all familiar with the outside of the police station, for they passed it multiple times every day on their way to and from their homes, but today they were wondering separately what the grim sandstone building would be like inside, because none of them had ever been inside its massive wooden doors. It was, after all, a police station, a detention centre, and its dark, permanently closed doors were an all too visible reminder of the weight and significance of what faced anyone unfortunate enough to incur, or stupid enough to flout, the duly vested enforcement power of the law.

III

"Checkmate in three moves."

"My arse!" The desk sergeant, Buckley, sat gnawing a rough edge of skin at the base of his thumbnail as he studied the board with an air of great and worried concentration. He was in trouble, and angry at himself for letting his young opponent trick him into sacrificing his queen—like a bloody schoolboy, was his thought.

The telephone rang, its shrillness echoing from the tiled floor and painted walls.

"Get that, will you?" Buckley muttered.

Harry Fletcher put down his sandwich and went to the counter, swallowing as he went. Buckley picked up his mug of tea and took a large swig, his eyes never leaving the chess board.

"Police station, Detective Fletcher speaking."

Buckley snorted to himself. Detective Fletcher! Not just Constable Fletcher. Christ, no. Detective C.I. bloody D. Fletcher.

"Yes, madam. Can I have your name, please? . . . Thank you. And your address? . . . Thank you. You say it's a nice one? No collar, but well trained . . . Your daughter? Fine. Can you bring it down here? Thank you, Mrs. Richardson. Goodbye."

Fletcher returned to the desk. Buckley still hadn't made his move. Fletcher smiled.

"What was all that about?"

"Hmmm?" Fletcher was already absorbed in the strategy of the board again.

"The phone," Buckley grunted. "What was it?"

"Oh, just some woman whose wee lassie brought home a stray dog. Says it just followed her home. Big one, though, an Alsatian. No collar. The mother thinks it's from a good home. Says it's clean and well groomed and apparently well trained. She's bringing it around."

"Mmm." Sergeant Buckley placed his fingertip tentatively on his one remaining bishop, his lips pursed.

"Not going to help, Sarge . . ."

"Damn it, I havena moved it yet! I'm still considering my options. Just you play your game and leave me to play mine."

"Just passing a comment," Fletcher murmured, smiling to himself.

"Well, I don't need your comments, thank ye!" The sergeant folded his arms on the desktop and plucked at his pursed lips, his brow creased. He had assumed the air of a man about to make a momentous decision when there came a clatter at the door and both men looked up to see three boys with golf bags over their shoulders, struggling through the double doors with a bicycle.

"Now what the hell," said Buckley, his voice rising rapidly. "Get that thing out o' here! Leave it outside. What d'ye think this place is, a garage?"

One of the boys looked at him in surprise. "But we found it! We're bringing it in to report it."

"Somebody must've stole it," said another. "It was hid in raspberries."

"Brambles," said the third boy. "They were brambles."

Sergeant Buckley threw a glance of sheer exasperation at Constable Fletcher, who was smiling slightly as he looked at the boys.

"And did it not occur to youse," the sergeant said, "that somebody might've hid it in there so that people like you couldn't find it and maybe steal it while he was goin' about his lawful business somewhere else?"

"No, Sergeant Buckley," said the first boy. "It was hidden all right, but it wasn't the owner who hid it. It was hangin' upside down, on the very top o' a big clump of bushes on the back road from the golf course, miles from anywhere. We think somebody stole it and threw it in there."

"Oh, you do, do you?" Buckley cocked his head. "How do you know my name? Do I know you? Och, are you not the Taylor boy from down the lane there? Your father has the factory?"

The boy nodded. "Yes, Sergeant."

"Aye. What's your name?"

"Barry, Sergeant."

"Barry Taylor, aye. And who are these two?"

"Greg Pearson and Andy McNeil."

"Aye, right enough, I know all three of you now. Ye're all from the same street. Well, let's have a look at this *stolen* bicycle, then. Bring it over here. Constable Fletcher, do we have any reports of stolen bicycles?"

"Don't think so, Sergeant, but I'll check."

"Aye, do that, Constable, do that." Buckley rose ponderously from the desk. "Now, let's see. It's a fine-looking machine, isn't it? Nearly new, I'd say. Where did you say you found it? Out by the golf course? Aye . . . Well, tell me again."

All three boys started speaking at the same time.

"All right, all right! Too many cooks. Young Taylor, you tell me. What happened?"

Barry related the whole story, and when he was finished, Buckley sat chewing on the end of his pencil. "Aye," he said finally. "You maybe did the right thing, at that."

Fletcher came back into the hallway. "Nothing on report, Sarge."

"The title is Sergeant, Constable, I'll thank ye to remember that. No report. I see . . . Not yet, anyway. Well, we'd better get a description of the thing wrote down on paper. First thing, though, I'll need the names and addresses of the finders."

"What for, Sergeant?" asked one of the boys.

"In case there's a reward for finding it. It would be a fine to-do if there was a reward and no address to send it to, wouldn't it?"

The boys, each aware of a whole pound note smouldering in his pocket, agreed that it would, and he wrote down the names and addresses of all three of them, after which he added the important details of their story and then turned his attention to the bicycle.

"Let's see here, it's a Raleigh, four-speed gears, with lights front and back, dynamo driven, caliper brakes, chain guard, kickstand, saddlebag—was there anything in it, by the way? In the saddlebag? No. I thought not. There should be a serial number on the frame, Constable Fletcher. Would you read it out to me?"

Fletcher did so, and then the sergeant read the entire report back to the boys. "Would you say that's right now, gentlemen? Have I missed anything out?"

Young Taylor spoke up. "Sergeant?"

"Yes, lad?"

"Just one thing."

"Aye? And what's that?"

"It's a lady's bike, Sergeant. There's no crossbar."

The sergeant's eyebrows shot up. "By the Lord Harry, you're right! Fancy me missing that." He added a note to the report, thanked the boys courteously, and sent them on their way. As they left, lugging their canvas golf bags, the last of them held the door open for a woman holding the hand of a small girl who, in turn, led a large Alsatian tethered by a length of string. The sergeant and the detective constable watched in silence as the woman approached the counter, where she addressed the sergeant.

"Are you Detective Fletcher?"

Buckley almost choked. Fletcher turned his head away. When the sergeant regained his voice, it was frigid. "No, madam, I am *Sergeant* Buckley." He emphasized the word by tapping his forefinger on the three stripes on his sleeve. "This," he went on, nodding towards Fletcher, "is Detective Constable Fletcher. Detectives are plainclothes police. They don't wear uniforms. Now what can we do for you?"

He knew very well what he could do for her, but his dignity was offended and so he let her tell the whole story as though he were hearing it for the first time. When the woman had finished, Buckley turned to the little girl. She was about six years old and looked very unhappy at the prospect of losing her newfound friend, who sat quietly by her side.

"Now, Jenny," he began. "That's your name, isn't it? Jenny?"

The little girl nodded.

"Well, Jenny, can you tell me exactly where you met the doggy?"

The little girl nodded.

"Aye." Buckley tried to keep his voice gentle. "Was it near here? Near where you live?"

The little girl nodded again.

"That's good, Jenny, that's good. Where was it, exactly? Can you remember that?"

Another nod.

"Where, then? You can tell me. It's all right. I'm a policeman."

"Tell the nice sergeant, Jenny," said her mother.

"Outside." It was the barest of whispers.

"Where? I didn't hear, dear."

"Outside."

Oh, Christ, that's just great, Buckley thought. "Outside where, Jenny?"

"Round the back."

He took a deep breath and reminded himself that this was a very young girl. He kept his voice very patient. "Round the back of where, Jenny?"

"Here."

"Hmm?"

"Here."

"Here? You— you mean round the back of the police station?"

The girl nodded.

"Can you show me where? Will you take me and show me?"

She nodded again.

Buckley straightened up and turned to Fletcher. "Keep an eye on things, Constable. I'm going for a wee walk with this young lady." He took her by the hand and, with mother and doggy in tow, they left by the front doors.

The child led them along the side of the sandstone building and came to a halt, pointing to where another wall, this one made of bricks, stretched out at right angles to the main one. It was the cellblock, with a row of narrow, barred windows high up under the eaves.

"There," Jenny said.

"What?"

The girl threw Buckley a look of purest scorn and pointed to the fourth barred window along. "He came through there."

"Oh, my Christ!" Buckley turned quickly to the child's mother. "Excuse me, Mrs. Richardson, I forgot myself."

***

Harry Fletcher had tagged the bike and wheeled it into the lost property department, and on his way back he met his relief in the hallway. Charlie Suckle—known to his colleagues as Honey—was three years Harry's senior in the force, but they were the same age and had grown up as friends and neighbours.

"Ah, Constable Suckle. It's about time you got here."

"Hi, Harry. What's cookin'? Anything dire and dirty threatening the safety o' the realm? Is there any tea ready?"

"Aye, I just made a fresh pot before we wis interrupted. Buckley's away wi' a wee lassie to see where she found a dog."

"What?" Suckle stopped in astonishment. "He left the desk? Are you kiddin' me?"

"No, honest to God! He went to see where she found the dog. She said it was right here." He paused. "Maybe I'll have a cuppa wi' you before I go home. Jeez, it's been quiet, though, except for the last half hour."

They went into the off-duty room that was little more than a cupboard with some kitchen chairs, a stained sink, and a small counter with a gas ring for boiling water.

Suckle poured himself a mug and stirred his tea, staring into his mug. "You made this?"

"Aye," Fletcher said. "What's wrong wi' it?"

"Too strong. I had to dig my spoon into it."

Fletcher picked up the big metal teapot with both hands and poured another mug for himself. It came out thick and almost black. "Aye, I suppose it is a wee bit stewed." He added two large spoons of sugar and some Nestlé's condensed milk from an open can. "Never mind, it'll put hair on your chest." He took a swig and sighed in deep appreciation. "Ahh! The lifeblood of the empire!"

"How come the woman brought the dog here?" Suckle asked. "Did she think we were the RSPCA?"

"I told her to. She lives right close by, and she's a widow woman. It'll save her traipsin' all over the country lookin' for its owner. 'S a nice dog, right enough. Somebody's worryin' about it right now, I'll bet you." He cocked his head, hearing a noise from the hallway. "That'll be Buckley back." Fletcher put down his mug and tilted his chair back so he could peer round the corner of the doorway, but then he scrambled upright and stepped into the hall. "What's up, Sergeant?"

The sergeant was alone with the dog and decidedly out of countenance. "What's up? What's *up*? I'll tell ye what's bloody up. *Sit!*" This last was to the dog, which promptly sat. The sergeant crossed to the phone on the counter and dialed a number. Fletcher leaned against the wall, wondering what had upset him. Charlie Suckle emerged from the off-duty room and nodded to Buckley.

"Evenin', Sergeant."

Buckley swung around to the two detectives. "She said it was well trained! Well, I'll tell you the whore's well trained! He's one o' ours, that's how well bloody trained he is! And the whore's runnin' loose, followin' wee lassies home! Jesus Christ!" He threw a venomous look at the dog, which yawned massively and lay down with his head upon his paws. "Well trained! Do you have any idea what could've happened? If that bloody dog had— Hello! Gibson? Is that you? I hope you're enjoying your new television, but I'm afraid I've a wee bit o' bad news for you. One o' your admirably trained dogs got out this afternoon. Aye, that's right, out! Wriggled out between the bars o' a cell window, probably lookin' for somebody to practise its chewin' on. But it followed a wee lassie home, instead!" He listened for about half a second and exploded again. "Jesus Christ! Am I *sure*? I've got the whore sitting right here in front of me! No, no' the lassie, the *dog*! . . . How the hell would I know which one it is? You're the bloody trainer! Get your arse in here, Gibson—smartish!"

He hung up, slumped into a chair, and pushed his fingers through his hair. "He says am I sure it's one o' ours? I felt like a right idiot when the wee lassie points right up to the cell window an'—"

He was silenced by a loud scream as the entrance doors crashed open and a woman half-fell, half-ran inside. She was dishevelled and wide-eyed with terror as she attempted to wrest herself free from the grip of the obviously drunk man who pursued her and had now seized her arm.

The dog was already up and crouched facing the newcomers, snarling, hackles bristling. Buckley jumped to his feet with an oath, sending the chair clattering to the floor, and the dog half turned to face him, ears flattened, snarling loudly, looking from the disturbance at the door to the new threat from the sergeant.

"Fletcher," Buckley snapped, his eyes on the tableau by the door. "Get that animal out of here. Take it to the cells. You there! What the hell do you think you're doing? Get your hands off that woman!"

The man had the woman by the shoulder and was trying to drag her backwards through the doorway. She was struggling, keening in a high, hysterical whine, and the dog sprang forward and crouched in front of them, fangs bared. The drunk sobered up very quickly and backed into the corner by the door, shielding himself behind the woman, who continued to keen in that high, terrified voice.

The dog still had the length of string around its neck, and Fletcher slowly approached the animal, reaching out to catch the end of the string, but the dog flashed its teeth at him with a vicious growl.

Buckley, his face set in a mask of determination, stepped out from behind his desk and made for the dog as though his sergeant's stripes would intimidate it, but the animal spun and darted towards him, fangs flashing. Buckley froze, and the dog backed away, tail down, and positioned itself so that it could see all five of them: the couple in the corner, the two detectives, and Buckley. Saliva drooled from its mouth.

"That dog's scared worse than we are." This was Charlie Suckle. "We'll never get near it."

Buckley stood stock-still and tried to speak in a calm voice. "It's responding to our panic. It's no' fully trained yet. That's why it was in the cells and not in the kennels. It's confused as well. Everything happened here just a wee bit too quickly. If we just stay where we are, wi'oot moving, and concentrate on relaxing, it might just relax the dog, too. Okay now," he said levelly, holding his voice to a friendly, conversational level. "Just relax, everybody. That's it. Relax. Missus, will you please stop makin' that noise? It's upsetting the animal. Please . . . Be quiet. You needna be afraid any more. You're in the police station, and you're safe, and we'll get your situation settled as soon as the dog calms down. But in the meantime, please stay quiet . . ."

The woman became subdued, though she still cringed from the man beside her, and for a long three minutes there was silence in the hallway. The late-afternoon sun shone down through the windows set high up in the walls and illumined the five motionless people watching the dog. And soon the dog stopped growling and slavering, though it remained wary and vigilant.

When Constable Gibson stepped in through the front doorway the dog spun to face him, and as Gibson said, "In the name o'—" Buckley snapped, "Gibson, curb that dog!"

"Tarka! Heel!" The dog rose instantly and ran straight to Gibson to sit by his left heel. Gibson reached down and fondled his ears.

"Gibson, get that thing back to the cells *now* and put it in a cage. And lock the cage." Buckley turned his attention to the couple in the corner. "You," he snapped, pointing at the man, who still held the woman in front of him. "Let go of her and sit over there. On that bench. Move, now, or I'll move you!"

The man did as he was told. Buckley went to the woman and took her gently by the elbow, then led her over to the chair by his desk. The man on the bench leaned forward, elbows on his knees, and put his face in his hands.

Buckley seated the woman and went behind his desk, righting his own chair and sitting down. "Now, missus," he said gently, "what's going on here? What happened?"

She started to cry, quietly this time. "He was trying to take my money. My handbag."

Buckley looked across at the man, his eyes cold. "Do you know the man? Have you ever seen him before?"

"Aye, he's my man . . . My husband."

Sergeant Buckley took a deep breath and squeezed his fingertips into the corners of his eyes as though rubbing the sleep out of them. His sigh was loud and eloquent. "I see . . ." He reached for a pencil. "Well, you'd better start at the beginning and tell me what happened right up to the minute when the two o' you came charging in here. Take your time, now. There's no rush." His voice was infinitely patient, infinitely weary. The man on the bench did not move.

The woman sobbed and then began to speak in a shaky, timid voice. "Well, ye see, Sergeant, he came home drunk. He'd been down at the pub since opening an' he ran out o' money. The boy told him I'd went to the store an' he followed me. But I need my money to buy food for the weans."

Buckley began making notes, and Fletcher and Suckle moved away towards the off-duty room.

Suckle checked his mug. "Bloody stone cold. Well, that was a right stewpot, wasn't it? I'm helluva glad Gibson arrived when he did, or we'd all still be out there!"

Before Fletcher could say anything, Gibson walked in. "What's goin' on in this place? What happened?"

Fletcher looked at his watch. "Sorry, Gibs, haven't got time to tell you. I promised Agnes I'd be home in time to get changed for the pictures and I'm late already. Charlie'll tell you."

"What you goin' to see?" asked Suckle.

"Haven't a clue, son. I just hope it's no' *The Hound o' the Baskervilles*. See yese all next time." Fletcher rinsed out his mug, took his coat from the hook behind the door, and made his way through the office. He didn't bother saying goodnight to Buckley, who was still writing up the domestic dispute, but he did notice one thing.

He turned on his heel and went right back to the off-duty room, shaking his head.

The other two looked at him in surprise. "You forget somethin'?" Gibson asked him.

"He hid the bloody board," Harry said. "The auld bugger hid the bloody chessboard! An' I had 'im right up against the wall. I mean it was checkmate in three moves. He was stymied! Down and out for the count! An' then a bunch o' laddies came in wi' a bike they found, and then that woman came in wi' the dog, an' right after that, like bingo, bango, bongo, the drunk man came in chasin' his wife, and the fly old bugger got out o' it again and quietly hid the bloody board! And now it's time for me to go home an' he's away tae England for a weddin' as soon as he gets off shift, and we'll never get to finish the game! When he gets back next week, he'll have conveniently forgot we even played, never mind that I had him beat."

"Christ Almighty," Suckle said, laughing at his friend's indignation. "You and your bloody chess!"

The Dry Smell of Potatoes

Nothing triggers memories and associations more instantly than the whiff of a once-familiar but long-forgotten smell. My grandfather was a lathe worker, known as a turner; a craftsman in a Glasgow machine fabrication shop where he spent his wartime days shaping and creating cylindrical steel engine parts to tolerances of thousandths of an inch. In the course of his work, his high-speed lathe was lubricated and kept cool by constantly flowing machine oil, and to this day the smell of warm machine oil will transport me back instantly into the hallway at the bottom of our stairs, where he stripped out of his boots and his workplace dungarees as soon as he came home at night. He died when I was eleven, but all these decades later that smell still reminds of Grandad and, amazingly, of another smell altogether: the eau de cologne he used when he had washed and made ready for his evenings at home.

In the town I live in today, we have a bulk food store called, unsurprisingly, The Bulk Food Store, and it features a partitioned-off area that holds nothing but spices. I never miss an opportunity to go there, even if it's just to stand there for a few moments savouring the smells. The overriding scents are cloves and cinnamon, cardamom and cumin, but the subtle undercoating of a hundred other fainter perfumes is always changing and always delightful. I come closer there than anywhere else to reliving the joy I took as a boy in visiting one particular store, The Wee Shop, in the village I lived in between the ages of eight and seventeen. I loved that little store, and you'll find it in this next story. But you'll also find an allusion to something else that was

going on at the same time: an inchoate, niggling sense of some brooding
powerful thing looming, threatening the peace and security of village
life in a way no one had ever experienced. Nothing had happened. But
the collective unease was a tacit acknowledgment that something was
out there, waiting.

"Could you give me a hand?"

"Sure, mister, no bother." The bus conductress leaned forward, offering her hand to help her passenger struggle from his seat as the bus entered the village square. Lachy Gordon always had trouble getting on and off buses. He had hooked the handle of his thick walking stick over his right forearm and was gripping the standing rail with his left hand, trying to pull himself erect, but the braking of the bus was pushing him forward as he tried to pull himself up, leaning backwards for leverage. The single-decker came to a full stop and the conductress pulled him up the last of the way, the strength in her arm surprising him.

"Wait a minute," she called to the people waiting to board. "Just hold your horses an' let this man off first."

The two ladies at the bus stop stepped aside as the conductress steadied Lachy and helped him down the steps, his stiff right leg with its surgical boot causing manoeuvring difficulties on the two high steps. One of the ladies sniffed as she looked at the big, expandable, solidly handled leather bag Lachy clutched firmly in one hand. It was a bulky, unyielding object—a portable desk, really—with a large white-enamelled metal plate attached to the flap and emblazoned with the legend "W.B. Thomson, Turf Accountant" in red and blue. When opened up and suspended from the bookmaker's neck and shoulders, it not only made a desk but functioned as a trademark, too, establishing the owner's bona fides as a businessman and setting him apart from the thronging racegoers known disparagingly as punters. No turf accountant attended a meet in the 1950s without his bag, and no bag was ever removed from a bookmaker's office unless it was taken to a meet.

The lady sniffed again as Lachy passed, careful to avoid soiling her clothes by being brushed against by a bookie.

It was a beautiful evening, late afternoon really, and Lachy was at peace with the world. He took his walking stick into his hand, inhaled deeply, and set out briskly, with his own unique rolling gait, in the direction of his employer's betting shop, throwing his right foot with its surgically booted clubfoot smartly out in front of him at each step so that he walked almost as quickly as a person with two good feet.

He had less than a hundred yards to walk and as he went he whistled under his breath. It had been a good three days; a fine meet! The book had prospered, and the previous night he had deposited a fat wad of notes into the night depository at the Bank of Scotland. He had spent the night in Glasgow, in an expensive hotel, the Grosvenor—the Gross Veenor, his fellow bookies called it—after calling his boss, Walter Thomson, to tell him they had done well and that the money was safe in the bank. He had told Watty that he would be home the following afternoon.

But for the first time ever, he had withheld information from his employer.

Lachy Gordon, for once in his life, had been lucky. On the first day of the race meet at Ayr, he had overheard a conversation in a hotel bar between two men who were obviously upper-crust and very well to do. Lachy, who had been a bookie's runner for years, had long since learned the folly of betting on anything, but there was something about this snippet of overheard information that excited him. *Fascinated* would be an even better word. He couldn't get it out of his head. He had had a strong gut feeling that what he had heard was absolutely straight from the horse's mouth, and that there might be collusion and illegality involved in it, but he had come across the information accidentally and no matter what happened afterwards, there could be no splashback that involved him, a nameless punter who had landed on his feet.

And so the following morning he committed himself in an uncharacteristic and totally impulsive splurge. He was carrying fifty pounds of his own money in his pocket to cover his expenses for the three-day meet and to buy his daughter a gift for her eighteenth birthday. That day at the track, using the nom de plume Sticker, he had split his fifty pounds among six other bookies, at odds of thirty to one, on a horse that was running the following day in the 2:30 race. He had then spent the remainder of that day fretting that, at the age of forty-nine, in the year 1955, he had done something really stupid, knowing as he did that the odds always, without exception, weighed heavily in favour of the bookies. Had that not been the case, Lachy knew, there would be no bookies. It was as simple as that, and you didn't need to be intellectually gifted to see it. For decades he had been unwavering in clinging to that truth, believing religiously that betting money on anything to do with sports—and most particularly horses—was absolute, wilful madness. And he had now set aside his beliefs and placed a large amount of his own money at the kind of extreme risk he deplored in others, based on an overheard whispered exchange between strangers.

For all the worrying Lachy endured during the hours that followed, though, the horse on which he had risked so much money romped home in a six-length lead over its closest challenger, and for the first time in his life, Lachy Gordon had walked away from a race meet with more than fifteen hundred pounds in crisp, folded cash of his own safely tucked into the money belt around his waist. He had earned as much money with that single coup as a fully trained doctor or lawyer would earn in nine months of hard work.

He paid his bill right after breakfast and checked out of the Grosvenor, the swankiest hotel he had ever stayed in, then spent two hours of the forenoon visiting his brother in hospital in the city, after which he passed another two hours shopping for something really special for his daughter. He found the perfect gift before two in the afternoon and ate a late-lunch omelette before catching the bus for home, his bookie's bag safely retrieved from the locker at the bus depot where he had stowed it.

The only sour note in his entire week had happened two nights earlier. Lachy had been enjoying a quiet supper—a pint and a hot meat pie in one of the pubs close to the racetrack—when he heard a roar of rage and the sound of a heavy, crushing blow. He looked up to see one man standing over another who was face down on the floor, bleeding and apparently unconscious. Ignoring the fallen man and the blood that seemed to be everywhere, the thug then reached across a table and grabbed a young woman by the front of her blouse. With his other hand raised and clenched into a fist, he hauled her towards him. Before Lachy could even move, the man smashed his fist into the young woman's face. The force of the blow spun her around and threw her backwards, but her enraged assailant wasn't finished. He struck her in the head and face again, several times in sharp, vicious succession. And then he straightened up and looked around, glowered at the stunned onlookers, and walked away, leaving her sprawled on the floor, her bare legs spread, exposing her crotch.

Lachy felt sick. He knew he couldn't have helped either of the victims, even if he'd had two good feet and a young man's agility, but to feel so useless was nevertheless deeply upsetting. He left the bar immediately, before the police could arrive—he was reasonably sure the attacker was a pimp punishing both his "property" and a business rival.

***

Lachy arrived back at work to find the usual few punters sitting in the traditional coal miner's crouch against the outside wall of the shovel—the miners' sardonic name for the betting shop where Watty Thomson shovelled their wages regularly into his bank account.

"Fine day for it, Lachy!"

Lachy agreed that it was, indeed, a fine day for it.

"How'd it go at the track?"

"We wiz just sayin' you might be comin' back in a fancy new car."

"By Jeez, youse bookies has the horses well trained!"

Lachy grinned at the last speaker. "What's up, Bunny? Your nag no' go?"

"Ah, shite!" Bunny spat onto the ground. "No' go? It went, all right, but it's still fuckin' goin'! The hoor hasna reached the post yet! They're sendin' oot the RSPCA tae look for it wi' a humane killer."

Lachy grinned and shook his head. "When are ye goin' to learn, Bunny? Ye shouldna follow the gee-gees that follow the gee-gees." Still grinning, he stepped into the betting shop.

The place was cool, dark, and empty save for Watty, who sat hunched over a desk at the back of the room. He looked up.

"Oh, there you are, Lachy. You're back."

Lachy approached the counter and heaved the big bookie's bag up onto it. "I'm just bringin' back the bag here, Watty, and we're done."

"Did you see your brother? How's he doing?"

"Fine, Watty, Calum's doin' fine. Doctor says he can go home next week."

"That's grand, Lachy. Do they know what was wrong wi' him?"

"Malaria. Can you imagine? He picked it up in Burma, during the war, but it hasna bothered him since, till he dropped in his tracks last week. Bloody lucky he never died. His next-door neighbour came round to sell him a raffle ticket and saw his feet stickin' through the scullery door, cried oot for the police. They whipped him into the Royal Infirmary. They don't know how long he'd been lying there before she found him."

"Bloody lucky he's got a nosy neighbour, then. She probably just stuck her neb up against the window lookin' for gossip. What's that you've got?"

Lachy had unbuckled the big bag and now held a small brown paper parcel in his hands. "Present for Fiona. It's her birthday."

"Already? Christ, Lachy, the years are fair flyin' by! What age is she now?"

"Eighteen."

"My God, she'll soon be gettin' married."

"Who to?" There was scorn in Lachy's voice. "No' to any o' the clowns around here, I'll tell ye! No' if I've got anything to say about it."

"Aye, ye're right enough there, sir. I canna' say I blame ye." Watty shrugged and went back to his figures, and as Lachy started to feel in his pockets for his cigarettes, the question came, as it always did, in a casual voice. "Everythin's okay wi' the accounts? Ye're sure?"

"Aye, Watty, I'm sure. Ye always ask me, and I'm always sure, and you always check the accounts yoursel' anyway, as they say, to make assurance double sure. That's Shakespeare, by the way. Macbeth. Have ye ever known me to be wrong wi' the accounts?"

"No, Lachy. But I always have to ask. That's why I'm the boss . . ." His voice tailed away, and then, "Seven thousand, nine hundred, ye say?"

"Aye."

"That's no' bad, no' bad at all. Ye done fine, Lachy. Thanks. Do I owe you anything for expenses?"

"Just what's listed in the book."

"Okay. Thanks again. You're a good man, Lachy. You can pick up your money before noon tomorrow."

"Then I'll away home and see what Fiona's got for the supper. Have ye seen her today?"

"No . . ." Watty was already poring over the books again. "No, she hasna been in . . . Cheerio, Lachy."

"Aye, cheerio." Lachy lit his cigarette, took his walking stick from where it hung on the edge of the counter, and went back outside. The loiterers had moved on, and Lachy stood on the steps of the shovel and looked around him. It was evening now, and the falling sun threw shadows clean across the street. He nipped the live coal from the end of his cigarette, took the pack from his pocket, and slipped the dog-end in among the few remaining cigarettes, smiling to himself as he did so. Fifteen hundred quid in his pocket and he was still saving dowps for later! He headed for Ogilvy's shop to buy another packet.

Jim Ogilvy was pushing up the sun awning over the store window as Lachy approached, and Lachy glanced at his watch. "Hey, Jim! You shut?"

Ogilvy peered back over his shoulder. "Oh, hello, Lachy. No, we're still open. Just rolling this up, now the sun's goin' down. Mrs. Ogden was telling me some young buggers ripped hers up the other night. Seems like they cut it wi' a knife. Bloody young hooligans. So I'm no' taking any chances wi' mine. Away inside, the wife's there."

Lachy stepped into the cool, delicious-smelling store, savouring the aromas of the place. He smelt the salty smokiness of the string-tied roll of rasher bacon hanging from the steel bar above the counter, and the different but equally smoky tang of the big gammon on the slicer, as well as the yeasty tang of fresh-baked bread and the dusty scent of black Indian tea leaves in the chest on the counter. The tiled back counter ran the width of the small shop and held trays of moulded butter pats, covered with squares of waxed paper, and wedges of creamy cheese, some still unwrapped. He opened the lid of the big bunker next to the doorway, looked in at the potatoes there and sniffed deeply at their distinctive earthy, dusty smell.

"Lachy Gordon, I've not got another customer who ever comes in here just to smell the tatties. Sometimes I think you must be either very special or just plain daft."

Lachy turned with a smile. "Hello, Mary. I'll admit I love the smell of them. They have a dryness when they're in the bunker that they never seem to have anywhere else. It's a . . . I don't know what it is, really. Just a special kind of scent. It's *evocative.*" He lingered over the word, then gave her a self-deprecating little grin. "Maybe even provocative. And listen to me wi' the big words! Anyway, I've never smelt anything else that comes close to it. I think I might buy a wee shop of my own someday, just for the smells."

"Aye, well, there's a lot more to it than smelling the stuff. It's selling it that's important, Lachy. What can I get for you?"

"Twenty Capstan, please."

Mary Ogilvy was a small, fat, cheerful woman with a smile for everyone. She placed his cigarettes on the counter. "That's three and fourpence. When did you get back?"

"Just got off the last bus." Lachy counted out the money onto the counter and then added an extra fourpence. "I'll need a box of Swan Vestas, too."

She placed the matches beside the cigarettes. "What happened to that lovely lighter Fiona bought for you? You never went and lost it, did you?"

"No, I keep it at home, just to be safe. We get some real quare fellows down at the shovel, an' wi' my luck one of them might just take a liking to it and stick to it."

"Aye, right enough. But still, it seems an awful shame not to use it. It's such a bonnie lighter."

"Oh, it gets well enough used, Mary, I promise ye. Was Fiona in this afternoon? What am I havin' for my supper?"

Mary frowned. "D'ye know, I havena seen her all day. I mind she came in yesterday afternoon and bought some sausages for Dick's tea, but she hasna been in this day, unless Jim served her while I was in the back. Jim!"

Lachy held up his hand. "It's no' that important, Mary. She'll have somethin' for her old father, even if it's only sausages frae yesterday. I'd better be on my way."

Jim was still struggling with the awning, which had stuck halfway up, and Lachy merely nodded to him and left him cursing like a trooper under his breath.

He made his way sedately home and turned in at the front gate. He smiled, anticipating the pleasure she would take in what he had bought for her birthday, as he limped along the path to the back door. It was unlocked and he went in.

"I'm home!" The house was silent. "Fiona?"

Lachy closed the door behind him and started to unbutton his mackintosh, fumbling for the light switch as he did so. It took him three tries to find the switch. He put his walking stick in the umbrella stand by the kitchen door, finally got his coat off and hung it up, and then reached for the note on the small message table just inside the door.

Had to go out. Might be a bit late. Put the kettle on. Love, F.

His smile faded as he began to wonder where she might be. It was unusual that Mary Ogilvy hadn't seen her, either coming or going, for there wasn't much of what went on in the village that Mary missed, and Fiona had never been the quiet, timid spirit who passed by any place in silence.

He heard someone outside, approaching the door behind him, and he opened it, but it was only the paper boy, dropping off the evening paper at the kitchen door. Lachy took the paper, nodded his thanks, and went back through the kitchen into the living room.

The vase of flowers on the table there was an explosion of welcoming colours. He limped over to the table, bent to inhale their fragrance, and then stopped. There was something . . . Something was different about the room. He straightened up slowly and looked around him. No, everything was the same as usual, and yet . . . What was it? The silence. His eyes went to the face of the clock. One thirty! The clock had stopped.

Lachy went to the mantelpiece and took the key from its place beneath the clock, opened the glass door over the face, and inserted the key in the first of the three holes. Eight winds, then on to the next hole. Eight more and then another eight for the last hole. The clock had a Westminster chime, and he and Emma had been given it as a wedding present by her parents. Winding it had become a ritual over the years. For him. No one else had ever touched the clock. He checked his pocket watch and then began moving the hands around the clock face with his fingertip, pausing at every quarter to allow the chimes to ring in their sequence. As he did so he stared at the wedding portrait of himself and Emma on the mantel, his mind going back to the day in 1938 when a runaway lorry had hurtled down a steep slope to smash into the side of the bus right at the spot where they were sitting. The accident had cost him his wife and the use of his right leg. As he thought about it, the leg began to ache.

Finally he was finished. He closed the glass door of the clock and stood there, holding on to the mantelpiece with both hands and feeling the pain swelling inside him again. After all these years it still hurt to think of it; not as often, now, thank God, but just as badly as ever. He shivered. The house was chilly.

There was a fire laid in the grate, even though the weather had been fine. Lachy bent down and put a match to the kindling, steadying himself with one hand on the front of the big fireplace, and then he reached behind him and eased himself back into the big old wingback easy chair. He raised his gammy foot onto the low stool and stared into the flickering, growing flames of the fire.

He sat there dreaming as the fire took hold on the coals and the room grew darker as the sky darkened outside, until the light spilling in from the kitchen was a bright pool reaching to the middle of the floor. The coals settled with a tiny crash and he started and blinked. He lowered his foot from the stool and rose to his feet, swaying a little until he was sure of his balance. Seven thirty. Fiona should have been home by now. Then again, he realized, she didn't know when to expect him. But still . . .

He stretched widely and yawned. It had been a long three days. The fire's heat felt good. He bent over the scuttle and threw on some more coal, and then he crossed to switch on the light and the radio, and he set the dial to the Scottish Home Service, and listened to Glasgow's radio comic family, the McFlannels. He'd missed the evening news, but that would be on again later. He looked at the clock again and picked up the paper, pulling a chair back from the dining table as he did so.

Half an hour later there was still no sign of Fiona, and he was allowing himself to get worried. He went back into the kitchen, filled the kettle, lit the gas jet, and put the water on to boil. As he turned away from the stove he noticed another piece of paper, lying on the floor in the corner. He leaned one hand on a chair back, swung his bad leg out behind him, and bent quickly to scoop it up, and his face creased as he read what it said:

Fiona—Sorry I missed you. No tea for me! I'm off on the ran-tan with a wee smasher! Might not even be home tonight!!! Don't worry, and don't tell Dad if he gets home before me. See you tomorrow, maybe, if I'm lucky. Dick.

Now what the hell? Lachy went to the message table, picked up Fiona's note, and brought it back to the kitchen table. Sitting down again, he looked at the two pieces of paper side by side, his brow wrinkled. What was going on? Dick must have left this note for Fiona yesterday, which was Saturday, and Dick always worked an extra four hours at the pit-head on Saturday afternoons, getting home around half past seven or eight o'clock. Friday was Dick's big night out. But Dick was twenty-two, big and ugly enough to look after himself, so he would leave a note for Fiona to ensure she wouldn't worry about him. She worshipped her big brother. But why hadn't Fiona tossed out the note? She wouldn't just leave it lying around for her father to find. And where the hell was she, anyway? Lachy found himself struggling against a formless, growing fear that made his stomach churn, and thoughts began swirling around in his head. He realized his hands were shaking.

Fiona had left a note for Dick on the message table. Why? Because she didn't expect to be home when Dick got home, right? Which would be about eight o'clock, right? Which meant any time now. Okay. He forced himself back to calmness and thought the entire affair through. Dick had evidently come home early the day before—Saturday—and left his note for Fiona on the kitchen table. Fine. Fiona had found it when she got home with the sausages for Dick's tea, read it, and left it lying on the table. But it had fallen from the table—probably blown off when she opened the door for something—and she'd forgotten about it. Then, this afternoon, she had had to go out for some reason and had left a note for whichever of them, Dick or her father, might get home first, which meant that she'd be home sometime around eight o'clock. Relief boiled through him and he relaxed.

The kettle was boiling and he rose and made a pot of tea. He set out his china pint mug with a spoon and the big sugar bowl on the table, and took the milk jug into the pantry. There was a brown paper package lying on the pantry counter. He picked it up and knew by the feel of it that it was the sausages Fiona had bought yesterday. Yesterday! Why hadn't she put them in the meat safe? A niggle of unease pinched at him but he brushed it aside and took down the bottle of milk from the shelf. Curdled milk slopped obscenely into the jug he held. Very carefully, Lachy set the bottle and jug on the counter and, his face like a mask, made his way to the kitchen door and opened it. This morning's milk was still sitting on the step.

Filled with dread now, he bent slowly and picked up the bottle, carried it back into the kitchen, where he almost fell into a kitchen chair. She must have been out all night! And all day today! Where could she be? Had something happened to her? What was going on? What could he do? His mind flashed back to the scene in Ayr, to that young woman probably not much older than his daughter, being battered and mauled by a hard-faced, merciless thug.

He was sitting there, wild-eyed, when Dick came barging in through the back door.

"Hello there! What's for eatin'? I'm starved!" He headed directly for the stairs to his room.

"Where've *you* been?"

Dick stopped in his tracks, surprised by the hostility in his father's voice. "What d'ye mean, where've I been? I'm just gettin' home from work."

"On a Sunday?"

"Aye. I stood in for a shift for Alan Matthews. His wife's expectin' their first any minute, and he wanted to be there when it happened."

"Where's Fiona?"

"Eh?"

"Where's your sister? And where the hell were you last night?"

Dick's brows twitched slightly. "Dad, what're you talkin' about? I don' know where Fiona is. She'll be about somewhere. What's the matter?"

Lachy found himself screaming. "She's no' about somewhere! She's no' here! She's missin', you selfish bastard. She's no' here and she hasna been here a' night last night nor a' day today. Yesterday's milk was sittin' soured in the pantry an' last night's sausages were still wrapped in the paper she brought them home in. Christ knows where she is and you're out whorin' around wi' some wee chippie ye picked up at the dancin'! Your sister's disappeared!"

"Jesus Christ!" Dick's face went pale and he sat down at the table opposite his father. "Now just wait a minute. Wait a minute, Dad. We're no' gonnae get anywhere screamin' and yellin' at each other. Now, are ye sure she's no' here?" He saw his father's face swell and he waved his hand to stop the explosion. "Okay, okay! You're sure. Fine. Where have ye looked?"

"I havena."

"You haven't looked? Then how do you know she's no' down at Maisie Elliott's house? Or over at Nance's?"

Lachy sat in silence, his hands lightly clenched on the table in front of him, his face the pallor of death. After a few seconds of stillness, broken only by the sound of the radio in the living room, Dick reached out and took Lachy by the wrist.

"Hey, it's all right, Dad. That's where she'll be, right enough. One place or the other. I'll go and get her right away. She's probably just got tied up and forgot what time it is."

"It's her birthday." Lachy's voice was a whisper.

"I know, I bought her a present. Did you?"

"Aye."

"That's great. Look, Da, her pals are probably havin' a wee party for her and she's lost track o' time. You stay here now and I'll pour you a fresh cuppa, then I'll go an' fetch her."

Fiona pushed open the back door and called, "Yoo-hoo! I'm here!" Both men froze. "I'm sorry I'm late but I've been wi' the girls. Did ye think I was lost? What's wrong?" Fiona said, looking at them. "What's the matter?"

Where the Sun Don't Shine

The original protagonist of this story was the first and only Mountie I ever met before I came to live in Canada. He was the closest friend of a cousin on my mother's side who had served with him as an infiltrator during the war, when the two of them, each fluent in French and German, were dropped by parachute, time after time, to operate in Nazi-occupied Vichy France, coordinating and consolidating the efforts of local Resistance groups. The cousin, whom I remember only very vaguely, was captured by the Gestapo in the city of Tours and never recovered from the torture he endured. He died less than two years after the end of the war, but during that brief time I met, and never forgot, his Canadian friend Henri, a former member of the Royal Canadian Mounted Police who, when hostilities ended, had opted to stay in Britain instead of returning to Canada and had taken a position with the City of Glasgow CID. He was my first real hero.

The last ambulance rocked out of the stony, litter-strewn lot and across the curbside, then swung away up the narrow street, bells clanging, and the crowd of onlookers slowly began to disperse, talking among themselves, comparing details of what they had seen and heard, and leaving the abandoned battleground to the police. The heads of the gallery audience in the open windows of the tenements across the street began to withdraw and the windows closed one by one, shutting in the life behind them and masking it with blank reflections of leaden skies and chill, drizzling rain blown on buffeting wind gusts.

One such gust blew a sodden newspaper against Finn Hudson's lower legs as he stood looking around him in the middle of the bombed city lot that had been the epicentre of the commotion. He muttered a curse and kicked out, dislodging the newspaper, the local *Daily Record*, which landed face up at his feet. His eyes caught the previous day's headlines and the date, Monday, December 5, and he grunted in disgust, realizing the following day, Wednesday, would mark the fourteenth anniversary of Pearl Harbor. It had been, in the words of President Franklin D. Roosevelt, a day that would forever live in infamy. Today, fourteen years minus a day later, he thought, he was witnessing another violent atrocity, this one in the city of Glasgow, thousands of miles from the Hawaiian Islands. This one, though, despite its closeness to Britain's once mighty shipbuilding yards, would not live in infamy; this one would be forgotten in a week, save in the memories of the few people directly affected by the deaths that had occurred.

A group of urchins who had been gawking, foul mouthed and profane, between the guardian bodies of the police cordon now started to re-enact the gang fight, swinging imaginary chains and knives and clutching at themselves in agony as they dealt and received crippling wounds. One of them slipped on the greasy, rain-slick cobblestones and fell heavily on one knee, and his obscene curses drew hard, jeering laughter from his companions.

A rusted tin can caught the eye of another boy and he trapped it beneath his foot as though it were a football and then flicked it deftly to his right, dropping it unerringly at the feet of his nearest neighbour, who began to dribble it, his arms extended shoulder high in the stylized ballet of the football player. In a matter of seconds, the rusting soup can clattering on the cobblestones became a soccer ball in the boys' minds and the dingy street became the green turf of Hampden Park. The fight they had been so avidly concerned with moments before was forgotten, and each boy clamoured for a pass. One of them yelled at the top of his voice, "Wee arra pee-pell!"

Detective Sergeant Hudson grimaced and turned the collar of his raincoat up as if it might protect him from the smirr of fine, dirt-laden rain that made the filth-blackened walls of the buildings around him glisten like sooty marble. *We are the people*, the yowling war cry of the Glasgow slum-dweller. He saw a late-arriving pedestrian hurrying towards the scene and recognized him as one of the cadre of reporters who wrote under the byline Pat Roller for the same *Daily Record* he had kicked off his leg moments earlier, and he walked away quickly, before the man could accost him. Hudson had nothing to say yet about this debacle, and he knew that anything the reporter could worm out of the neighbours would be far more acceptable to his readers than the toneless comment he might be lucky enough to get from a member of the Constabulary.

Hudson paused before he stepped onto the pavement—he was Canadian and it had taken him a long time to accept that the "pavement" was actually the sidewalk in the UK—and looked back again at the bombed lot, taking note of the grim drabness that surrounded it and sucking reflectively on the enormous-feeling space in his right upper jaw where he'd had a molar removed the previous week. The gum still felt smooth and slick and raw.

There weren't really all that many bomb sites left in Glasgow that hadn't been completely rebuilt in the decade since the war, he knew, but this one had been permanently abandoned. Accessible to wheeled traffic only from a narrow alley in the rear, built for horse-drawn wagons in the days of Queen Victoria, the site had been condemned, deemed unsuitable for redevelopment, from the night it was levelled by an errant trio of jettisoned bombs intended for the Clydebank shipyards. It was now one of the bleakest and most hopeless patches of wasteland in Glasgow, partly due, he suspected, to the garishly flaunted modernity of many of the buildings flanking it. Most of the city's unsalvaged bombed-out sites, he knew, were here in this district known as the Gorbals, where teeming thousands of people jammed the slums near the industrial wilderness that lined both banks of the River Clyde and the shipbuilding yards that had attracted the German bombers.

Barely an hour earlier, the police had arrived here to find six bodies strewn like bloody bundles of rags; six neds, as the local hard men were called. All were well known to the police; all of them belonged to the same gang and all were bleeding like stuck pigs. There had been no sign of their assailants, but no one had the slightest doubt who the attackers were. The Chisholm family members who lay scattered on the ground had had it coming for a long time. The locals called them the Chisels, for their sharp-edged hardness and their deep-cutting methods, and everybody knew that when they got it, it would be from the Reilly crowd. Hudson sucked his gum again, probing the empty, raw socket with the tip of his tongue, and let his eyes roam around the lot.

Whoever had planned the attack had done it well. The Chisels all worked together on the docks as stevedores, four brothers and two cousins, and this brick-strewn place of ruin was on their normal route home. This afternoon, though, they had walked into a carefully laid ambush. Hudson supposed it was understandable that no one had bothered to inform the police until it was all over. Why spoil a good fight, after all? But even in a city notorious for its gang warfare, this fight had been epic in its savagery. Hudson, who had thought police work held nothing new for him, had been astounded to see that one of the men writhing on the ground had been transfixed by a four-foot *katana*. A samurai sword, for Christ's sake! No doubt salvaged as a souvenir of some Asiatic battlefield and smuggled home to grimy Glasgow in the kitbag of some undersized, kilted Jock to remind him of his days of glory. Another man had a garden sickle embedded in his neck, just below his right ear, with the hooked point pressing the skin outward on the back of his neck. The others might recover eventually, but at least one of those two was almost bound to croak, and that would run the butcher's bill up to murder. The Reillys had really gone in over their heads this time. Hudson spat through his teeth. *We are the people!*

A police car glided to a halt at the curb beside him, its rear door swinging open, and he heard his boss's voice from inside. "All right, Hudson, let's go."

He climbed in through the door held open for him, squeezing clumsily past the occupant's knees to collapse heavily into the deep leather upholstery.

"Carry on, driver." The detective inspector looked quizzically at Hudson. "What's the matter with you, then? From the look on your face there, I thought you'd lost a pound note and found a penny. Hudson?"

Hudson blinked and grimaced. "Sorry, Inspector, I was dreaming."

"Admirable ability at times. Dreaming about what?"

"The Comanche."

"Beg pardon?"

"The Comanche. They spoke of themselves as 'the people.'"

"What the hell are you talking about, Hudson?"

"The American Indians, sir, the Comanche. They believed they were the chosen people of God."

"So do the Jews. And so have millions of other people throughout history, for all we know. What's that got to do with the price of coal? Are you all right, Hudson?"

"Sorry, Chief, you haven't a clue what I'm on about, have you? I was thinking about the shout 'We are the people.' I think the Comanche at their worst were more civilized than some of the animals we have to deal with every day."

"Oh, is that all? For a minute there I thought you were cracking up. D'you mean that's the first time that thought's occurred to you? About the Indians, I mean?"

"Yeah, I guess it is."

"Amazing. You North Americans are so bloody naive."

"Canadians, Inspector."

"I said *North* Americans. Had I meant Yanks, I should have said so. Anyway, it's all the same thing, isn't it? Not British, that's the thing—"

Hudson cut his superior off with a raised eyebrow. "Not British, Inspector? Forgive me, but that seems to be a bizarre comment from someone whose name is Sabatini."

"Cheeky sod! One of these days you'll try my patience, Sergeant Hudson. No, but really, it has long been my considered opinion that Attila's Huns would have fared badly against our Glasgow keelies. That's why the Scottish Regiments have always been the shock troops of the empire. D'you know what the Germans call the Glasgow Regiment, the Highland Light Infantry, stationed on the Rhine? Call them the Poison Dwarves. Isn't that delightful? The Poison Dwarves." He savoured the sound of it. "Rolls off the tongue just lovely, doesn't it?"

"Appropriate, I'd call it," Hudson murmured. "But keelies is a strange word. I know it means thugs, but where did it come from?"

The car swung around a corner and Hudson was thrown against Sabatini's shoulder. He apologized and pulled himself erect with the hand strap.

"Means thugs now, but it didn't always," Sabatini answered. "The original keelies were the labourers who worked in the shipyards—Irish, most of 'em—laying down the keels of the big ships. Long before the trade unions came along the keelies were a law unto themselves: tough, independent, and beholden to no one. No one messed with them, not the shipowners, the yard owners, or the other trades. By association, over the years, the name's come to mean ungovernable toughs."

The driver had switched on his wipers to combat the suddenly heavy rain, and Hudson looked through his side window at the drab street they were on, the ground floors of the dreary, soot-stained tenements lined with small, dingy, watery-looking stores. The pavements were strewn with waterlogged refuse.

"Look at the state of this place, sir. Bonny Scotland!"

"Oh, come on, Hudson, that's hardly fair. You must have some pretty seamy cities in Canada."

"Not in the west, sir, and not like this."

"Yes, well, it's all so new over there, isn't it? No traditions, no history. Just try to remember that this place is a lot older than your Edmondsville."

"Edmon*ton*."

"Aye. Edmonton. That's what I meant. Just bear in mind there were people buying things in these shops when people in Edmon*ton* were thinking about cutting down trees to try and build a shelter from the rain."

Hudson sighed. "I hope Edmonton never gets as bad as this."

"Oh, it will. Just give it time."

"Where are we headed now, sir?"

"Back to the station, to regroup and wait."

Hudson responded to that one like a bear to a goad. "Wait for what, for Chrissake? We know who we want. Let's go get the sonsabitches."

"Calm down, Sergeant, and do try and keep a civil tongue in your head." Sabatini nodded towards the young driver.

"Sorry, Inspector. Sometimes . . ."

"Aye, I noticed. Sometimes your enthusiasm gets the better of you. Some people I know would call your over-exuberance insubordination. Luckily for you, I am an understanding fellow who can make allowances for colonial lack of *savoir faire*." He looked out the window at the almost deserted sidewalk, a half smile on his face, and Hudson felt, not for the first time, a surge of liking for his crusty but good-natured boss.

"Anyway," Sabatini continued, "there's no point in going off half-cocked. As you say, we know who we're looking for. But where do we start looking? Damn city—any city, for that matter—is a rabbit warren, and we're just a couple of ferrets. The Reilly neds have split up long since. By now they could be anywhere from the docks to the Trongate. But we've every man on the force looking for them. They're not overly gifted wi' brains and they'll turn up sooner or later, and when they do, we'll collect them. Meantime, there's no point in running around like—"

The car braked savagely, skidding, almost dumping both of them on the floor.

"What the *hell*?"

"Reilly, sir!" the driver cried, both hands clamped on the wheel. "Big Paddy. Across the street. In front of the tobacconist's."

"Jesus Christ, it *is* him!" Hudson had the door half opened. "Follow him, Hudson! And for God's sake don't lose him. We'll get on the blower for help and cut him off at the end of the street."

Hudson was already out of the car and starting across the street when he heard another squeal of outraged brakes and a Glasgow Corporation double-decker skidded to a stop within a foot of him. He rested one hand on the front fender as he leaned forward to make sure that nothing else was coming. But Reilly was gone already. He must have seen the police car and ducked into the covered close that gave access through the tenement block. Hudson took off at a run, cursing the slickness of the wet cobblestones and almost falling into the entrance of the close, where he stopped for a second, trying to hold his breath as he listened for running footsteps. Nothing. Halfway along the passageway, the stone stairs to the upper floors rose to his right. He could see the exit to the courtyard ahead of him and his mind raced. If Reilly had gone up the stairs they had him, even if he had friends in one of the apartments. On the other hand, he might be gambling, crouching on one of the landings above, waiting for Hudson to leave by the courtyard so that he could head for the street again. Hudson barely slowed down as this sped through his head, but he knew his man, and Big Paddy Reilly would never run and hide. He wouldn't risk looking frightened. Hudson bared his teeth and sprinted for the back exit.

The courtyard extended the full length and breadth of the block and was surfaced with hard-packed crushed cinders, littered with piles of rubbish and fringed with patches of green where sparse clumps of rank grass and malnourished dandelions fought for life. The entire space was criss-crossed with a maze of drying lines and clothes poles, one suspending a bedraggled, soot-streaked wash that someone had forgotten to save from the rain. To his right, next to the communal middens, a long row of brick wash houses bisected the courtyard, stretching all the way to the far end of the yard, where it abutted a ten-foot-high wall of crumbling brick topped by a quadruple strand of barbed wire. Beyond the wall was the gable of a factory or warehouse.

Hudson saw all of this in one sweeping glance. He also saw Big Paddy Reilly launch himself from the end of the farthest wash house roof, grab hold of the barbed wire on the top of the wall, and haul himself up and over and out of sight.

Cursing a blue streak, Hudson ran to the nearest midden and stepped onto a dustbin to climb to the roof of the wash house beside it, knowing that the straight line of wash house roofs was the most direct route to where Reilly had jumped, but he misjudged his first step and his foot slipped into a morass of soggy tea leaves and rotting potato peelings. Cursing even more fluently, he got his balance back and placed his foot more securely on the rim of the garbage can, threw his weight forward, and launched himself upwards. The dustbin tipped under his weight and fell over noisily, but he had enough purchase on the edge of the roof to haul himself up and onto his feet.

His raincoat was tight around his legs as he ran flat out along the hump-backed roofs of the row of wash houses, leaping over foot-high flues all the way and twice having to clear four-foot spaces between buildings. Finally he stopped, shrugged out of the coat, dropped it on the roof, and then he was off again.

As the high wall at the end of the yard drew nearer, he could see that it was one hell of a long way out and up to the top of it. Reilly had done it, sure, but Reilly had probably taken the time to stop and gauge the jump. Now if he took the same time, Reilly would be long gone, and suddenly he was at the jumping point and there was no time to do anything but jump. He put everything he had into his legs and leapt out and up. His right hand grabbed the top strand of wire and his left slapped the rounded cement top of the wall as both his knees smashed hard into the bricks. He gritted his teeth against the wave of pain as his boots scrabbled for purchase in the brickwork. One foot found a hold and he heaved himself up towards the top. The rusted strand of wire in his hand was threatening to sever his fingers and he suddenly knew he wasn't going to make it. He cursed the truth of it but made one last, Herculean effort. His head cleared the wall and his eyes swept the yard beyond it.

It was a builder's yard. Nothing moved. He saw a judas gate hanging open in the gate at the end just as his weight began dragging him backwards, and he let go of the wire and fell, landing with his knees flexed and his back to the wall. He straightened and leaned back against the wet bricks, his heart thumping violently.

Even as he started rubbing his left thumb along the tender insides of his right fingers, he was looking around for some means of getting over the wall, and there, lying on its side along the wall of a wash house, was an old ladder. In less than thirty seconds Hudson was over the barbed wire and on the wall. Looking down on the other side, he saw piles of planking and scaffolding stacked haphazardly everywhere, and directly below him was a huge mound of wet sand, showing two deep scars where Big Paddy Reilly had landed. Hudson dropped into the sand pile.

The judas gate opened on to a cobbled lane between high walls. To his left and farther away on his right were two more big yard gates, each with its own judas entrance, both of them closed. Hudson did a mental coin toss and chose the gate on his left. He stepped into a small, dark yard. As he did so, he was scared half to death by a sizzling crack of lightning directly over his head that deafened him. His nostrils and chest filled with the stink of ozone, and he froze there in the entrance to give his wildly thumping heart a chance to slow down. He was beginning to wonder for the first time where the rest of the Glasgow City police force were. And then, in the preternatural silence that followed the thunderclap, he heard a whimpering coming from the partially open door of a shed to his left. He moved towards the sound cautiously, willing the sagging door not to creak as he pulled it open enough to allow him to look inside. He didn't see it at first in the gloom—just inside the door, a black Labrador bitch was suckling a litter of pups on a pile of sacking. She roused and came for him, snarling and shedding pups from her teats like bloated black leeches. He backed out quickly and slammed the door shut.

Outside in the lane again, almost growling with frustration, Hudson made his way along to the next gate. It was locked. He cursed under his breath and stepped back, and as he did so, he saw the wet sand on the sill of the judas gate. He grinned, his lips pulling back in much the same way that the Labrador bitch's had.

The gate was high and flat-fronted, offering no foothold. Lightning flared again and thunder crashed simultaneously, and rain began to fall in earnest, heavy drops bouncing back up from the cobblestones. In a matter of seconds Hudson was drenched but utterly absorbed in trying to find some way of getting through or over the obstacle in front of him, and then he heard a lorry coming along the lane. It was a big three-ton Bedford, and an idea came to him. He ran to flag it down. It braked to a stop beside him and the driver stared down at him in amazement, rolling his window partway down.

"What the eff's goin' on? Are ye daft? What's up?"

Hudson silenced him by flashing his warrant card, just the way they did it in the American movies. "Detective Sar'nt Hudson. Glasgow City CID. I need to get on the roof of your cab so I can get over that gate and into the yard. Pull over there."

"What for?"

"I haven't got time to explain. Just take your truck over by that gate and let me get up on top."

"Jesus Christ, I'll open the effin' thing for you."

Hudson blinked. "What?"

"I said I'll open the effin' gate for ye!"

"You got a key?"

"I hope so, it's my effin' yard! How come *you* want into it?"

"There's a wanted man hiding there."

"Away, for Chrissake! How'd he get in through a locked gate? Has he got wings, maybe? Can you no' get in the same way? Or did he maybe stop another lorry an' jump up on it?"

"Look, fella," Hudson's voice changed dramatically, becoming softer, calmer, and somehow far more threatening. "I told you, this is police business. Now will you get out and open that goddamn gate?"

"Are you sure you're a polisman?" The driver squinted at him. "You don't look like one. Polis don't have crew cuts. You look more like a Yank to me."

"I'm a Canadian, mister, and you've got a fugitive hiding in your yard, or escaping through the front. I don't know how he got through your goddamn gate but he did, and if it turns out he's got a key you're gonna be in some deep shit. You hear me?"

"Okay, okay, stand oot o' the way." He put the big truck in gear and pulled over to the gate, where he got out and produced a heavy bunch of keys from his pocket. He was reaching for the padlock when Hudson stopped him.

"Not the big gate, just the judas."

"But—"

"No buts! Do it!"

The man unlocked the judas gate with a Yale key.

Hudson caught him by the biceps and pulled him back. "Okay, I'm going in. You haul your arse down to the end of the lane, quick as you can, and look for the police. Tell them where I am. There'll be lots of them around."

He opened the gate quietly and stepped through, hearing the man behind him begin to run along the lane. He closed the gate and looked around him, taking in the details of the yard with a sense of déjà vu. At the far end, a narrow passageway led between two rows of outhouses to a door in the back wall of a derelict-looking building with broken, rag-stuffed windowpanes. He had never seen it before, but the sense of familiarity was strong in him, and then the explanation came to him. There was no real resemblance, but the atmosphere reeked of the same kind of danger that had been present in another backyard, in France, in the city of Tours, eleven years earlier, in 1944. He had entered the same way back then, and had found a pair of Gestapo thugs waiting for him. He squeezed his eyes shut, trying to erase the vision and the memory of the pleasure he had taken in killing. That was then. This was now. He was in Glasgow, Scotland. No Gestapo here.

He crossed the yard in nine long strides and drew level with the open doors of the first two outhouses. The insides were stuffed with rubbish, and Hudson gave them only a cursory glance. His gaze was riveted on the door ahead of him, and he moved forward slowly now, placing his feet carefully so as to make no noise. He was reaching for the doorknob when two things happened simultaneously. He heard the sound of someone rushing at him along the passageway at his back, and the door in front of him was pulled open suddenly to reveal Big Paddy Reilly standing just inside, a length of heavy chain in his right hand.

Hudson dropped one shoulder and lunged at the huge man in front of him, catching him by surprise full on the breastbone, driving him backwards into a third figure close behind him in the unlit hallway. Hudson kept driving, giving neither of them any time to recover, bulling his way past them and breaking free into the interior, where he swung back to face them, the three of them silhouetted against the dingy grey light from the open door. One of them fumbled against the wall and switched on a light, and then all three stood motionless, looking at Hudson as he crouched in the middle of the almost empty room, holding a short police truncheon of heavy ebony wood in his hand, his wrist securely threaded through its leather loop. For several seconds they remained in tableau: nobody moved or spoke. Then Reilly broke the silence.

"What are you goin' to do wi' that?" He nodded derisively at the truncheon. "Are you goin' to beat us all up and take us down to the polis station on your own?" His two companions began moving slowly away from him, circling left and right, their eyes fixed on Hudson. One of them, a skinny, pasty-faced six-footer, held an open straight razor, the classic weapon of the Glasgow thug. The other, who looked to be no more than eighteen, had a long-bladed, double-edged military-issue commando knife in his right hand, and Hudson could see that he was quite familiar with the feel of it. Hudson's eyes flicked from one to the other and then to Big Paddy, and he felt the dry, coppery taste of fear beneath the edges of his tongue.

"Call them off, Reilly. Don't even think about taking this any further. You're caught, you're out, and you're in trouble enough. It's not as if nobody knows who you are, or who I was following when I jumped out of the car." He saw Reilly's brow crease slightly, a flicker of anxiety in his eyes, and he kept talking. "You did see the car, didn't you? You know I wasn't in it alone."

Reilly blinked.

"Call these guys off. This place'll be crawling with coppers any second now. In the meantime, one of these clowns makes a move on me and you're all for the high jump. As it stands, I'm taking you in for questioning in regard to the matter of a civil disturbance earlier today. That's all. But keep this shit up and I'll nail your Irish ass to the wall. You've never done hard time, Reilly. Why start now?"

"Fuck off, copper!" It was the youngest of the three, his voice barely more than a whisper but the hard, nasal accent of Liverpool unmistakable. "Just 'cause you're some kind of Yankee tough guy, yer don't think we're goin' to fall down dead of fuckin' fright, do yer? How fuckin' styoopit d'you think we are? We know what you want, all right. We know what you're gonna fuckin' get, too." He kept moving as he spoke and Hudson had to turn his head slightly to follow him, while trying to keep the tall, skinny one in his line of sight at the same time. It was impossible.

"Get the bastard!" Big Paddy swung his chain up and leapt forward. Hudson threw himself backwards, almost tripping over a wooden chair. He was off balance for less than two seconds but he grabbed the toppling chair in his one hand and flung it underhanded into the face of the young thug. The razor man was very close, too, his arm up to slash, and Hudson lashed out in a backhanded chop, catching him square on the wrist by sheer luck and sending the razor flying.

"Mind!" yelled Big Paddy, swinging his chain high with two hands, waiting only for a clear target. But just as he hesitated at the top of his swing, a police whistle shrilled and a heavy thumping of feet came from the open door behind them. Reilly in alarm turned towards the sound, and as Hudson began to straighten up he saw, from the corner of his eye, the young Liverpool thug flying at him from his left. Hudson half spun, his left arm going straight out to ward off the attack, his right, with the truncheon, whipping up with all his strength behind it towards the head of his assailant. He felt the shock of contact through his wrist, and then the weight of the man's body sent him flying backwards again to crash against the wall. For a fraction of time he thought he was looking at a photograph: the young thug was caught in a falling attitude, forward and sideways, his head thrown back and his eyes wide, and Big Paddy was staring wild-eyed at him as he fell. Police were pouring through the door and he tried to stand, but found himself having difficulty.

As though from miles away he heard Reilly shouting, "You cunt! You stupid cunt!" Hudson's vision started to blur and he found himself looking down in surprise at the hilt of the kid's black commando dagger protruding from his chest. His hand started to move towards the knife, but it was a long way, and then he felt his face hit the gritty floorboards, and he was surprised that it didn't hurt, because it should have, and yet he was still falling down a long, deep black well.

***

He woke up in a white-painted room, the sour taste of vomit in his mouth and a face with steel-rimmed spectacles inches from his own.

Pain raddled him as blackness came again, and people far away were calling his name, and he wanted to open his eyes and be back in Alberta, back in the bush, but they wouldn't let him go. He opened his eyes and there was still a face inches from his own. This time it was a woman's. And behind her, looking down over her shoulder, someone else, someone familiar. Sabatini! How in the hell had they got Sabatini? Pain again, and the blackness coming back . . .

He awoke next time to the sound of utensils tinkling on a passing trolley and followed the nurse with his eyes as she went along the ward.

"Well! Rip Van Winkle has rejoined us."

He turned his head slightly and there was Sabatini, sitting by the bedside, grinning at him. He swallowed, trying to clear his throat, then spoke, but nothing came out. He collected himself, breathing deeply and fighting down his panic, and tried again, and this time was able to generate a whispered croak. "Inspector. What's up?"

"You are. Or you will be soon, they tell me. How are you feeling?"

He considered that, breathing deeply several times, and then nodded, or tried to. "Okay," he said softly, instinctively careful. "I guess . . . What's going on?"

"How d'you mean?"

"What am I doing here?" He moved to sit up and gasped as a tongue of pure agony flared around his rib cage.

"Steady on, Hudson! You won't be able to move around much for another week or so, according to the quacks."

"What quacks? What happened?"

"Do you remember what we talked about when I was here yesterday?"

"You were here yesterday?"

"Well I'll be damned! You spoke to me for about half an hour yesterday, and I would have sworn you were fully rational at last."

"At last?" Hudson closed his eyes and drew a deep breath. He   · waited for the pain to die down to the point where he could speak again. "Inspector, I haven't a clue what you're talking about."

The inspector was sitting on a hospital chair, legs crossed, his raincoat folded over his lap, and he examined his fingernails with a musing look on his face. The thought crossed Hudson's mind, as it had before, that Sabatini was the cinematically perfect senior British police detective.

"One of Big Paddy Reilly's villains stuck a shiv in you. Almost made a job of it, too. An inch or so to the right and you'd have handed in your papers there and then. As it was, it was touch and go. For a long time nobody thought you were going to live."

"Christ! I remember now. He came at me from the side. Big Paddy was throwing in the towel. Did you get him?"

"We got them all. We picked up the rest of the gang within twenty-four hours. Trial's next week."

"Next week! Jesus, that's fast."

"No, not particularly.

"Not *particularly*? Oh, shit. How long have I been here, then?"

"About three weeks."

"Jesus!"

"Aye, He must have been here with you, because you wouldn't have got this far without Him."

Hudson frowned. "Do we have a good case against them, for a conviction?"

"Aye, laddie, the best. There's never a doubt. We did have a . . . small procedural problem. Garnet, the sod that stabbed you, he died. You smashed in his right temple." He held up his hand. "Don't even ask. Clear-cut case of self-defence against three villains resisting arrest with lethal intent."

"He was just a kid. Couldn't have been more than eighteen."

"Forget it. He was a right sod, an unbelievably evil young bastard. A professional killer. The Liverpool force had quite the book on him, and believe me, nobody's sorry you killed him."

"Did anyone find my coat?"

"Your coat?"

Hudson sighed. "My new raincoat. I had to take it off when I was chasing Reilly. It was slowing me down."

Sabatini shook his head. "No coat picked up as far as I know. Some slummy must have been lucky."

Hudson thought for a few seconds, then said, in a flat, emotionless voice, "Inspector, you can take your Bonny Scotland and shove it where the sun don't shine. I'm going back to Canada."

"Back to the home in the west?" Sabatini sounded unimpressed.

"That's the sterling truth. You can take it right to the bank!"

"Oh, it's no' as bad as all that, lad. We might find you a juicy murder out in the countryside somewhere. Get you some nice fresh air and the scent o' the heather. Better than a holiday."

"Bullshit, Inspector Sabatini."

"Aye! Well. I'm glad to see you're feeling a bit more like your old self." Sabatini stood up. "I'll be back in tomorrow. Is there anything you'd like me to bring you?"

"A one-way ticket to Edmonton, Alberta."

"Don't be bitter, son. You'll feel different once you get a wee bit better."

"The hell I will."

"We'll see, we'll see. Cheerio for now." Sabatini headed for the door.

"Boss? Thank you for the thought. But about changing my mind? Remember what I said. Two words, both capitalized: Bull, Shit."

Hudson closed his eyes. He could already feel the excitement of boarding the ship.

The Ides of March

Between 1956 and 1958 in Scotland, in that area of the County of Lanark known as the Clyde Valley, abutting the southeastern border of the city of Glasgow and stretching south and east in the heavily populated region of the valley, people went about in fear of the homicidal depredations of an unknown, untraceable madman who was killing people wantonly, and apparently taking great pleasure in doing so. His first victim, a girl named Anne Kneilands, had been found bludgeoned to death, but not sexually molested, on a golf course near the village of Blantyre in 1956, and as her murder was quickly followed by others, it became clear that whoever the killer was, he lived locally and had been active in the area for some time.

He was eventually identified as Peter Thomas Anthony Manuel, a resident of the village of Viewpark, close to Glasgow, who had been raised Roman Catholic, bearing the names of three great saints. He was hanged in Barlinnie Prison in Glasgow on July 11, 1958, after being found guilty of at least seven first-degree murders, though he certainly committed nine.

Manuel was born on the same day as me: March 15, the storied ides of March that saw the murder of Julius Caesar, and he was thirty-two, fourteen years older than me, when he died. I remember being stunned when I found out that he had been arrested as the prime suspect in the killings, because I had known the man for more than five years. I didn't know him well, but I knew him well enough to call him by his name—Peter—and for him to acknowledge me when we met.

Familiar with my high school uniform, he had recognized me as a fellow Catholic the first time we met, and we had spoken civilly to each other on many occasions, usually when we would encounter each other casually at the local bus stop, waiting to catch a bus into Glasgow or East Kilbride. In those days in Scotland, anti-Catholic discrimination was still open and unapologetic, only the rich had cars, and everyone else went everywhere by bus or, for distances more than ten or fifteen miles, by train.

Peter Manuel's arrest and trial had a radical effect on me; more than one, in fact. In listening to the radio and reading reports and transcripts of the trial, I had my first brush with astrology, discovering that Manuel, like me, was a Piscean. Nothing remarkable there, you might think: one in every twelve other people in the world is a Piscean. At that time, though, I knew nothing at all about astrology and so I went on to read a newspaper summary of the typical character traits of people born under the sign of Pisces.

What I read scared the hell out of me. I recognized the nascent similarities between myself and the homicidal monster who had been terrorizing the county for years before he started killing people. He was intuitive, intelligent, charming, imaginative, artistically creative, and personable when he wanted to be. He was easily influenced by others and by his own perceptions of what people expected of him. He was also volatile and unpredictable, with an addictive personality that made him easily susceptible to alcohol and drugs. He was subject at times to an inability to appreciate realities, displaying a pronounced tendency to self-delusion, and occasionally appearing to live in an imaginary world of his own creation.

I discovered to my horror, in reading that article, that I possessed all of those same attributes, in spades, and was already a heavy smoker by my mid-teens, and I now know it would not be far off the mark were I to claim that Peter Manuel was one of the most powerful influences in my early life. There was never any question of any desire on my part to emulate him in any way, but the absolute reverse of that became a constant in my early life, because I could never forget how seductively likable the man had been, and I was repelled by my own failure to look past that facade and see how unutterably evil he had been beneath that charming, ingratiating surface. No one else had seen it, either, but that nugget of commonplace wisdom evaded my recognition for a really long time. And so for years, whenever I faced a life choice of any magnitude, I would ask myself what Manuel might have done had he faced the same choice, and then I immediately chose the opposing option.

I was never able to write about him, despite the trauma that merely knowing him casually had caused me. I tried, at various times later in my life, but I couldn't do it. In 1956, and even in 1966, Manuel stood alone in my mind and in the minds of my contemporaries as the twentieth-century Scottish murderer. There had been others, but they barely had significance to us in central Scotland: Jack the Ripper, Mary Ann Cotton, and Amelia Dyer, along with the acid bath murderer John Haigh and the banally evil John Christie had all been English, a pertinent detail to Scots in general and particularly so in the 1950s. Scotland's notorious bodysnatchers, Burke and Hare, had been the most heinous Scots of recent times, selling the corpses of their victims to anatomical researchers, but the era of the bodysnatchers had ended in January 1829, when William Burke was hanged. The Scots, since then, had thought themselves well rid of the shame of such a thing.

From my more personal perspective, though, Hitler and Stalin had killed on an epic scale that was simply unimaginable: Peter Manuel, on the other hand, had been the fellow next door, and I had known him.

The two pieces that follow are all that remains of what I thought, or what I wanted to say at various times, about the madness of a multiple murderer.

I. Recon

School was out, and chaos held sway where it always did at that time of day. The hands on the Aldersyde Town Hall clock showed 4:27 and the main bus stop at the circular town hall junction was a seething mass of people of all ages fighting one another for access to the already crowded red buses that arrived and departed in an endless line. Two harassed transit inspectors fought valiantly but in vain to keep the jostling crowd in order, fully aware that there was no way to assert any kind of control. The nose-to-tail parade of buses pulling up to the stop sign were all bound for differing destinations, and as each pulled in, it attracted a crowd of passengers from the throng surrounding the two narrow gates in the waist-high steel railings.

The inspector who stood in the gutter beside the first gate had his hands full just trying to control the jostling, noisy schoolboys who lined the railings at his back peering eagerly at the fronts of the buses that sat in line waiting to pull forward. All of them were hoping to pick out their own bus and steal a march on all the other waiting passengers by squirming through the railings and getting on board ahead of everyone else. The inspector's cap was jammed down firmly over his forehead, and he clutched a clipboard in his hand, looking as though he would dearly love to use it to clip the wings of some of the more unruly members of the crowd.

His companion, who could have been his twin brother in the long-coated, peak-capped black uniform they wore, had an even more thankless task. His duty was to keep the second opening in the railing— the one intended for disembarking passengers—unobstructed so that the people getting off the buses could make their way directly to where they were going. His job was made utterly impossible because most of the unloading passengers were only changing buses, and this particular intersection was the changeover point for most of the bus routes that converged on the town.

This confusion, repeated every weekday, was primarily caused by there being three high schools in the vicinity, one Protestant and two Catholic, and each afternoon they poured somewhere in the region of eighteen hundred students and staff into the streets at four o' clock. And almost all of them travelled to and from school by bus.

The real root of the troubles, though, lay in the fact that the hour-long daily chaos started in Johnstown, five miles to the north, which also housed two large high schools: a Protestant public school and a Catholic girls' convent school. The buses from Johnstown were already crammed when they arrived in Aldersyde.

The drivers and conductors called the back shift—the stretch from 10:00 a.m. until 6:00 p.m.—the Purgatory Patrol. The day shift, on the other hand, which brought the students in each morning, was nowhere near so nerve-racking. It was known as the Funnel Force, since the incoming passengers poured from the buses en masse, quietly and sluggishly, prompting one waggish inspector to earn a degree of fame on the buses for describing the morning process as "the daily enema." The back shift, however, everyone agreed, was hellish.

One other element fed and sustained the daily maelstrom, and it was sex. The changeover bus stop was, over and above all else, an adolescent lovers' trysting ground. Every day of the week, the intermediate and senior boys from St. Thomas More Catholic School hung around the bus stops for the extra twenty minutes it took for the buses carrying the girls from St. Catherine's Convent School to reach Aldersyde from the next town, and that twenty minutes allowed the students from Aldersyde High public school to walk the extra distance from their school to the town centre. The Aldersyde High students were all Protestants, so they had no girlfriends among the convent girls—inter-religious amorous relationships were the highest form of taboo—but they were healthy, virile, and sexually repressed young males, and they loved to look and lust, since conventional Protestant wisdom stated that Catholic girls, once released from the domineering, sexually oppressive influence of priests and nuns, were insatiably promiscuous.

They would all have been astounded to know that the Catholic boys believed exactly the same of Protestant girls, since none of those ever had to worry about the trauma of the confessional and the admission of sexual transgression to a priest.

And so the crowded changeover bus stop had become a temple to adolescent lust, or at least to frustrated agonizing, between the hours of 4:15 and 4:45, five days a week. For the Catholics, the venue represented the only opportunity most of them had for social intercourse away from the eyes of parents and overseers. For the wide-eyed Protestant boys, the bus stop had the allure of a red-light district for a sailor; and for everyone involved, the place and the daily extravaganza had the heady aroma of freedom—from regulation, from school, from supervision. The Bus-Stop Bean Feast was the most exciting half hour of the school day.

The regular participants in the daily rites had their own arrangements and territorial preferences. Small groups waited in designated places around the central scene, some in front of the few shops that lined the approach to the main street junction at Aldersyde Cross, half a block from the bus stop, others in front of Bianca's Café across the street from it, and still others against the fence around the corner on Larkhall Street, the quiet side street that ran alongside the town hall. The boys would arrive first and await the arrival of the convent girls from St. Kit's, who poured from their buses and made their way to their various assignations to spend ten or fifteen minutes conversing and flirting with their admirers, before splitting up and making their ways homeward.

By five o'clock each day, the junction was deserted.

***

The girl belonged to a group of three, and he had chosen her very carefully several weeks earlier. She was pert, vivacious, and perfectly proportioned, with a superb pair of breasts that kept boys hanging round her in slack-mouthed, glassy-eyed wonder. Her two friends were attractive, too, one of them, a bright-eyed redhead, far more classically beautiful than the others, but the pert one was the star of the trio. She had an alluring, not-quite-unconscious air of sexuality, and it radiated from her like some kind of magnetism. Her skin and her complexion were flawless. Her eyes wide-set and startlingly blue beneath the black Irish hair that fell around her shoulders in what looked like a solid sheet of silken ebony. She had wide, soft-looking lips, bright red with no need of lipstick, and her teeth were white and even and flashed when she laughed, which she did often. He knew her name was Patsy, and knew that some of the other girls, jealous of what she had, called her Patricia, conveying their disapproval.

He stood on the island in the middle of Larkhall Street, right at the junction where it joined the main road. At his back was the iron Victorian railing surrounding the subway entrance to the ladies' public lavatory. The entrance to the underground gentlemen's toilet lay twenty yards behind him, but he had no worries about seeming conspicuous standing by the ladies'. Here he could stand and look at the girl of his choice from a distance of less than twenty feet, without fear of being noticed, too far away to hear what she was saying, except when she laughed and raised her voice—and even then all he heard most of the time was her tone, not the words—but close enough to watch her mouth and to read the hungry expressions in the eyes of the boys who surrounded her.

Like her friends, she wore the dark blue blazer and knee-length skirt of her school uniform, with a pale blue blouse and regulation dark blue and silver striped school tie. Her legs were robbed of any individuality by the uniform's dark blue knee socks with twin silver stripes around the top, and plain, sensible black shoes with laces. Catholic school uniforms were not designed to emphasize the siren in girls. And yet this girl transcended the drab uniformity. Even beneath the shapeless blazer, twisted out of shape as it was by a shoulder satchel crammed with books, he could see the thrust of her breasts; their fullness and the ripeness they offered the hungry eyes of the boys.

Tits, he thought. *Not breasts. Those are tits!* He had seen them, even. He had followed her the previous Saturday to the Odeon cinema, where she had met her two friends and removed her coat to display—and there was no other word for it—display a pink fluffy mohair sweater, tight and tit-hugging, its bottom tucked firmly down into the waistband of her skirt so that her shameless wantonness was flaunted openly, attracting boys like bees to a sticky jam jar.

He had followed her in and managed to get a seat directly behind her, four seats in from the wall in the back row. By the time the newsreel and the trailers had run, the three girls were sitting apart, the spaces between them taken by boys. By the end of the second reel of the first feature—"the wee picture," as opposed to "the big picture" that was the main feature—the boy on her right had put his arm around her, his hand resting on her shoulder. The hand had stayed there for the entire performance, but he had felt himself grow hard, leaning forward casually to sniff at her hair and imagining the thoughts that were swarming in the mind of the boy, feeling his lusts and what the boy wanted to do, knowing that the fool was unconscious of what was unfolding on the screen, obsessed by the softness that lay just beneath and beyond his spread fingertips.

He had been forced to pull away and sit back when the girl straightened slightly and raised her hand to her hair at the back, as though sensing his closeness, and he had glanced casually towards the wall, just in case she turned to look. The seat next to him was empty, but the people in the last two seats against the wall were in a huddle and his view of them was blocked by the broad shoulders of the man, twisted sideways in his seat. He turned his head slightly sideways and watched for a long time from the corner of his eye, fascinated, as their passion gradually made them less and less discreet. The woman's knee came into view, nylon-clad, bracing itself against the wooden back of the seat in front and then falling away, sideways, with a flash of white thigh as the man shrugged around even further, his elbow moving forward as his hand gained access.

The man's shrug had twisted his body forward, clear of the seatback, leaving a gap, and now, his heart pounding in his throat, the watcher leaned back, as casually as he could, and risked looking directly. Beneath the man's right shoulder he saw the underside of a white breast below disarranged clothing and then the brief, disappearing flutter of a white handkerchief and the spastic, agonized stiffening of the man's whole frame. The watcher, eyes wide, nostrils flaring, caught the merest hint of wet, sexual body smells and then it was he who went rigid. Hands clasped seemingly demurely in front of him, he sat motionless as ecstatic bursts of erotic electricity surged through him. When it was over, he was utterly spent, his eyes on the screen now, his mind empty of everything except the dwindling of his passion, the wetness cooling on his thigh, and the itching of the sweat beads that had broken out on his upper lip.

As he watched the girl now, the group around her began to disperse, its members waving to each other and moving away as she made her way towards her own bus stop, flanked by her two companions. Glancing quickly in both directions just to make sure no one was paying attention, he picked up the attaché case at his feet and crossed the street, catching up to the three girls as they approached the bus stop, which was now almost deserted. He glanced up at the town hall clock. It was 4:45. The girls' bus pulled in on time, and he boarded with them. The girl called Patsy caught his eye and hesitated, a tiny frown of almost-but-not-quite recognition passing across her face. She started to smile, but perhaps thought better of it when he gave no sign of knowing her, and she walked forward to her seat.

After she got off the bus, he stood up and waited for the next stop, a couple of hundred yards farther on. He shrugged out of his raincoat and folded it over his arm, and carrying his case, he walked quickly back to where he could see her coming towards him. She was walking fast with her head down, seemingly oblivious to her surroundings. He was no more than thirty steps from her when she stopped at the waist-high brick wall edging the garden of what must be her home, and she looked around in a mildly startled way as though she didn't know where she was. He kept walking, careful not to look at her directly as she bent forward over the gate and lifted the latch. The hem of her skirt rose barely an inch at the back of her knees, but he saw the flesh and his mind registered it before she stepped through and closed the gate behind her.

He slowed his pace and watched as she approached the door of the house and reached for the handle, but before she could grasp it the door swung open and a uniformed police sergeant emerged. He promptly stepped aside, holding the door wide for her and smiling in welcome.

"Hi, Dad," he heard her say as the policeman pulled her to him with one arm and kissed her forehead. "How come you're home in the middle o' the afternoon?"

"Just came back for something I forgot," the sergeant said. "Cheerio." He squeezed her again, then ushered her into the house and closed the door behind her. He barely registered the man passing the garden gate.

The man's heart was racing and he fought an overwhelming urge to run. He had no idea if the policeman was following him and he did not dare look back. How could he not have known the silly bitch's father was a policeman? But until that afternoon he hadn't cared who her father was, or her mother; all he had been interested in was what her body would feel like when he finally laid hands on her. Only now did he begin to see that there might be complications attached to what he wanted to do.

Was the man behind him?

He forced himself to walk more slowly as he saw the bus stop ahead, his ears and nerve ends straining to detect sounds of movement at his back. When he crossed the road and reached the stop he made a show of leaning indolently against the sign as he looked back casually the way he had come, and his entire body sagged when he saw there was no one in sight but a solitary woman, washing the front windows of her house and paying no heed to him at all.

Breathing deeply then, he bent and set his case on the ground, then put his raincoat back on. He buttoned it partway and shrugged until it sat comfortably, looked around him again, then took a comb from an inside pocket and ran it through his hair with the polished confidence of a man who doesn't need a mirror to help him look good. Satisfied to be fresh-groomed again, he replaced the comb and checked the tightness and alignment of the flawless Windsor knot in his tie, making sure it sat carefully in the exact centre of his starched shirt collar. That done, he checked his watch. The next bus would take him back into Aldersyde and anonymity. As for the Patsy bitch and her slutty ways, he would see her again the following day.

II. The Censor

He thought of himself as the Censor, knowing that Cato the Censor had been one of the greatest and most highly regarded citizens of the Roman Republic before the time of Julius Caesar. But Cato the Censor, for all his insistence upon guarding the morals of the state and its citizenry, had been more directly concerned with traditionalist morality and the extirpation of political corruption and excesses in the Senate—a different kind of censor altogether, in this modern one's opinion, from what was needed in this day and age, and while he had great respect for Porcius Cato's censorial integrity and achievements, this twentieth-century successor to the title saw himself as fulfilling a more closely defined but equally necessary function, and he pursued that function with great and unflagging diligence.

Below him, on the mossy road at the bottom of the slope, the two young people he watched through a filtering screen of leaves reached a bend that would take them out of his sight. He moved to follow them quickly, crabbing sideways along the sharp crest and craning his neck to keep them in view. But his foot slipped on the greasy soil, still slick from a shower that had fallen half an hour earlier, and he fell. Grasping wildly at the rough bark of an elm tree in an attempt to regain his balance, he toppled backwards from the ridge, the skin of his fingers tearing against the bark, and the side of his face whacked solidly against the bare clay of the bank. He began to slide, and he wrenched himself around until he lay face down, scrabbling for a hold, digging wildly with fingers and toes and knees at the ungrippable soil and leaf mould. For more than twenty feet he tobogganed, gibbering in panic until he ended up with a thump against the bole of another tree.

He lay there for some time, eyes screwed tightly shut as he struggled for breath, spitting dead leaves and soil out of his mouth and cursing in a furious undertone as his heart pounded and pure adrenaline surged through his bloodstream. Eventually he calmed, and then, after another several minutes, he opened his eyes and slowly raised his head. He was facing diagonally uphill, and he could see his cloth cap about twelve feet above him. There was a sharp pain under his ribs, and he groped beneath himself and found he was lying on the case for his binoculars. Remaining flat, he fumbled further, seeking the glasses themselves, but they were gone, and he remembered that he had been holding them when he slipped. The heavy binoculars must have slid on down the hill all the way to the bottom. He spat out more grit and turned with extreme caution to look down behind him, making sure that he moved in no way from the tree that anchored him.

The tree was rooted on the brink of the river gully. The edge of the cliff was no more than two feet from where he lay sprawled, and from there the ground dropped almost vertically for thirty feet to end in a bank of shale, eroded boulders and debris, all overgrown with a tangle of rank, green grass overhanging the edge of the swift-flowing river. It was not a big river—less than twenty feet wide, in fact—but it was fast and it roared loudly over its boulder-littered bed.

His binoculars were right there, in full view, and he cursed again, his voice flat and vicious. They hung, snagged by their leather strap, from a gnarled tree that protruded from the cliff face ten or twelve feet below him. Slowly, he moved his head to look up at the sky through the branches, seeing bright patches of blue among great fluffy masses of grey-white cloud. A gust of wind rattled along the gully and he felt it chill the damp mud on his face. He spat again, putting a world of disgust into the gesture, and began to manoeuvre himself upright until he could sit with his back against the tree trunk and look himself over.

His hands and clothes were caked with mud. There hadn't been much rain, just a shower, but enough to moisten the top layer of soil until it was like sticky ice. He rubbed his palms together hard to dry the mud on them and flake it off, and he considered his situation. His cap was above on the slippery slope; his binoculars were below, hanging from the cliff face. He looked along the slope to his right and then to his left, gauging the terrain there to be the easier way out. He stood upright slowly, his back to the tree, and carefully checked the distance to his cap. Then, glancing all around him again before starting, he spat once more and set about inching his way upwards, towards the cloth cap.

It was hard going. For every two feet he advanced, he slipped back one. He used his toes like wedges, kicking them into the soft, yielding, loamy earth as hard as he could, willing them to be anchors for his weight. Eventually, after a long, slow progress, he decided he was close enough to the cap to make a lunge for it. He threw himself in an upward dive and his fingertips snatched the cap by its peak, clutching it tightly, and then he was sliding down again, faster with every second. This time, however, he was prepared: he swung his right leg violently backwards, rolling over so that he almost sat up, and then lunged towards the tree on the edge of the drop. His arm snapped around the bole and he pressed his face to the bark, shuddering and gulping violently, winded and scared spitless.

Moments passed, and he became aware that his heart had slowed down again and his breathing felt normal. The side of his face was still pressed against the rough bole and he suddenly noticed a richly coloured, evil-looking earwig on the bark a few inches from his face. From the closeness of his viewpoint the craggy, moss-covered bark took on the dimensions of a range of hills and the insect seemed as large as a dinosaur, its burnished-burgundy body armour gleaming and the polished amber fork of its tail menacing and awful. He jerked his head away. It was only an earwig, he told himself, but still he shuddered as if someone had walked over his grave.

"Fucking thing," he whispered. "Ugly bastard!" He snapped off a piece of dried twig from the tree trunk and skewered the earwig, watched it wriggle and writhe. His face twisted in the semblance of a smile as the insect bisected itself and the pieces fell away, but even after it had gone, he continued to stab at the bark with the twig and to stare at the spot where the earwig had been. And then the twig snapped and his knuckles scraped against the bark. He became absolutely still for several seconds. Then he stood upright again, his arm still around the tree trunk, and sucked gently on his skinned knuckles as he looked around him.

To his right, there was nothing but sheer cliff. Along the edge of the drop to his left was a scattering of small trees and saplings, and he could see that by swinging and scrambling from one to the next, using them as anchors, he would be able to reach a point about a hundred yards away, where the cliff below seemed to have more of a slope to it. He would be able to get down there, but it was a very long way away. All around him brightness grew suddenly and he felt the welcome warmth of the sun. He looked up. The clouds were widely scattered now and the sun was blazing down. It would not take long for the slope above him to dry at this rate, but then, he thought, even dry, the hillside was steep and there were no footholds, and the thought of skidding back down, and maybe over the edge this time, made him shudder.

He looked down again, searching for his binoculars. They were still there, hanging from where they had snagged.

He gazed at them, seething as he fingered the strap of the empty case hanging around his neck, and then he looked around for something he might use to dislodge the glasses, but even as he looked he knew there was no chance of finding a dead branch close enough to reach. The only thing around him that wasn't mud or solid timber was tree roots. His eyes narrowed at that thought and he looked back down, then leaned forward very slightly to examine the face of the cliff beneath him. It was not rocky but composed, like the slope above him, of loose, friable shale and soil, with boulders here and there. The entire face, however, was covered by a network of protruding tree roots, looping lengths of them sticking out everywhere like the rungs of a rope ladder.

His insides began to churn with an almost sexual excitement at the danger inherent in what he was about to do. He would go down the cliff using this natural ladder, and he would collect his binoculars on the way! The more closely he looked at the roots, the more convinced he became that they would support his weight easily. He couldn't see many beyond the halfway point of the descent, but he could see that by the time he got down that far, he would be able to drop free and scramble the rest of the way in safety.

He stooped to tuck his trouser legs into his socks, and then he straightened and took off his trench coat and his jacket. He wadded them into a large ball and dropped them over the edge of the cliff, watching them as they fell into the long grass at the bottom. He started to remove the case for the binoculars from his neck and then hesitated, struck by the possibility that it, too, might end up snagged by the roots on the cliff face. He left it where it was, safe around his neck, let go of the tree trunk, and lowered himself gingerly to the edge of the drop, sitting for a time with his legs dangling over as he mapped out a route to the bottom. There was a big, strong-looking loop of root directly beneath him that was a perfect first step. He turned onto his belly, took his weight on his hands, and eased his body out and down. His searching toe found the root and he tested its strength carefully before trusting it with his weight. It gave slightly and then held firm and he lowered his whole weight on to it. It was fine—wobbly, but just like the rung of a rope ladder. He took a handhold on a smaller root and with painstaking care began to make his way down the cliff face.

Five roots later, about nine feet down, his luck ran out. There was an ominous ripping sound as the root he had chosen tore away from the bank, and he was thrown sideways, grabbing for a handhold and finding none, his fingers missing the big loop above him by inches. When the root had given way, the case around his neck had fallen behind another root, and as his fall swung him backwards the leather strap twisted behind his head. Now it clamped tight around his throat as he dangled there. He tried to scream, but couldn't, and then the leather strap broke and he fell.

***

He became aware of the sound of a blackbird singing somewhere close by, and water running swiftly over a rocky riverbed. He opened his eyes and saw blue sky, partly hidden by a canopy of green leaves. He saw the dark face of the cliff above him. Very carefully, he sat up, and then, surprised that he had succeeded without pain or difficulty, he started testing his arms and legs, tentatively at first and then with more and more confidence as he realized everything was working. There was nothing broken at all, but his clothes were in a terrible mess.

It was only when he tried to stand that he realized what a pounding he had taken. His entire body seemed to be one massive ache, and his head was thumping so percussively, he feared for a moment it might split wide open. Wincing in agony, he stood up slowly, his arms spread to counteract his dizziness, then painstakingly made his way to the waterside.

He sat on the grass and removed his shoes and socks, placing them carefully well away from the edge, then lowered his feet into the water, gritting his teeth against the icy shock of it and hating the sensation of cold bottom-mud squishing between his toes, trying hard not to think of leeches. The mud lay only underneath the bank, where there was no current to speak of, and his first step took him out of it, onto a clean-swept floor of sand and pebbles. Two steps farther out, still short of the point where the water began to roil as it picked up speed among the rocks, he dropped to his knees in the shallows and ducked his head into the chilly water. His trousers were soaked, as were the front of his shirt and his sleeves up to the elbows, but he felt much better. He washed his hands and his face and then slowly climbed back to the bank and hobbled painfully on cold and tender feet, carrying his shoes and socks, to where his coat and jacket had fallen. Beside them, as though he had placed them there carefully and safely, lay his binoculars, evidently having fallen straight down the cliff. He hefted them in his hand as he checked for damage and then looked up at the cliff to where the case that had almost hanged him now hung, lodged behind the treacherous root, its broken strap dangling for about six feet.

His face twisted into a snarl and he whipped back his arm and threw the binoculars savagely up at the case. They fell short and slid back to his feet in a shower of earth and small stones, and he picked them up again, muttering to himself, and brushed them roughly with his sleeve before setting off to walk awkwardly along the narrow strip of land by the river's edge. He was on the wrong side of the river now, separated from his quarry by the swiftly flowing water, and so with no other options, he moved slowly and cautiously over the uneven, stony ground, looking for a place to cross safely.

He had only gone about ten paces when he bent to pick up a broken branch of aged-looking wood, about two inches thick and five feet long, that looked straight and strong. He tested it, attempting to bend it like a bow between his hands, and when it refused to bend, he took a firm grip on it. Holding it in front of him like a blind man's cane and using it to test the bottom at every step, he struck out across the river. He carried his trench coat in a tightly wadded ball, holding it well clear of the water, its buttons fastened to make a container for his rolled jacket, his cloth cap, his shoes, their toes stuffed with his socks, and, tucked securely into the middle of all that, his binoculars. The coat's knotted arms secured the package one way, while its belt secured it the other, and he had thrust his arm through the belt as far as it would go so that the package rested snugly over his shoulder, lodged against him in the hollow beneath his jaw.

The broken water began about seven paces out, and he eyed the wavering line along its edge with wary trepidation, noting the daunting speed of the flotsam that spun by in the spating current and trying to see beneath the surface to the boulders that littered the river's bed beneath boiling, turbulent mountains of spuming whiteness. The footbridge he would have crossed had he stayed on the crest of the hill as he had planned was several hundred yards downstream, and for a moment he considered returning to the bank and walking down to it. But he couldn't say what might lie hidden from him to obstruct his passage along the base of the cliff, and so he filled his lungs with a resolute gulp of air and stepped forward with one foot. The current clutched at him violently, threatening to swing the outstretched leg around and back into the shallows. He planted his stick firmly and pushed his foot forward and down to the river's bed. His leg immediately forced the water's rush upwards and the iciness of it in his blood-hot crotch sent him staggering helpless, digging in panic with his other foot to find a solid stance and jamming his bare toes painfully against a hidden rock. With a rising howl of anguish, he threw out his arms, releasing his stick, windmilling for balance, and fell forward.

The package on his shoulder fell free with his sudden lurch. His arm disappeared to the shoulder in heaving froth as he snatched it up again, and he skinned the knuckles of his clutching fist against another hidden stone, but somehow he managed not to fall in completely. Rigid with pain and fury, he remained braced on the tripod of his legs and right arm, still gripping his sodden trench coat as the waters swept around him, and then he heaved himself erect again and bent his head back, releasing a scream of hatred and frustration to the sky. Then he whirled and flung himself back towards the riverbank, thrusting violently through the shallows now, kicking his legs through the water, uncaring in his rage that the few remaining patches of dry clothing were being soaked by his splashing progress.

He threw himself down on the bank, tore apart the sodden bundle, and savagely thrust one foot into his sole remaining dry sock and shoe, then he wrung out the other sock, pulled it on, and jammed his foot into the wet shoe. He snatched up the remnants of his bundle and strode grimly towards the river again. This time, though, he pushed forward without stopping and made it safely to the other side, to the wide, well-trodden footpath that the young couple had used. Wasting no time in trying to salvage his condition, he set off immediately, hurrying left along the path and muttering constantly to himself as he walked, as though he were upholding both sides of a conversation. Once out of the sun, it was almost cold in the shade of the trees, and his wet clothes stuck to him, chilling him, raising gooseflesh on his arms and legs. Water squished in his sodden shoes and he kicked viciously from time to time at the long grass that edged the path. But when he reached the turn in the path where he had last seen the couple, their footprints were still distinct in the moist softness of the ground.

After a while, the riverside path widened considerably and wound away from the shade of the trees. He stopped, looked around him to be sure he was quite alone, and then struck off through the woods until he intersected a faint game path. He followed this for about half a mile to a wide clearing like a water meadow, filled with long grass. He stopped there, his teeth chattering with cold, glad for the sun's warmth, and then he walked on until he reached a pile of large stones that lay almost in the exact centre of the woodland meadow. Another broad pathway passed within yards of these stones, and he peered carefully in each direction. Satisfied that no one was around, he lowered himself to the grass and began to wrestle out of his wet clothing. His underpants were still fairly dry, so he kept them on, but he wrung the water out of his socks and trouser legs and spread them with his shirt and undershirt on the rocks to dry in the sun. He undid the bundle and set out his coat, jacket, cap, and binoculars on the warm rocks. He reached for his jacket and drew from one of the pockets a glossy black watertight tin containing cigarettes and a box of matches.

He lay back, enjoying the warmth of the sun, dragging on his cigarette, listening to birdsong and the muted sound of the distant river, wider here and not so fast flowing. He reached again into a pocket in his jacket and drew out a big old-fashioned railwayman's watch. It showed 2:30. He took a grubby kerchief from his coat, picked up the binoculars, and spent the next several minutes polishing them, spitting on the leather grips to moisten the dried earth that encrusted them and then scrubbing at them until he was satisfied that he could get them no cleaner. Finally he breathed on the lenses and polished them lovingly, then flicked his cigarette-end in the direction of the river. He checked the glasses again, critically, and when he was satisfied they were as clean as they could be, he slipped them carefully into the folds of his jacket, lay back on the grass with his cap over his eyes, and fell asleep.

***

The sun went behind a cloud and the coolness awakened him. He sat up irritably, fumbled the watch from his pocket again. The sky was largely hidden by one enormous cloud. He got up and checked his clothes. The shirt was dry; the rest were drying quickly. He turned them over and went back to where he had been sitting, lit another cigarette, and smoked it slowly, caressing it with his fingertips. When it was finished he stubbed it out in the grass and lit another. The sun was shining again and he stretched his arms, enjoying the freedom of being almost naked. He started to lie back again but then reached over for his trench coat, dug deep in the left pocket, and came out with a wilted bar of Cadbury's Dairy Milk. The paper wrapping had disintegrated, but he knew the chocolate would be undamaged. He ate it two squares at a time and licked the last crumbs from the wrapper, and then he screwed the wrapper up into a ball and threw it at a thrush that had been watching him for several minutes. The bird took off immediately, swooping low towards the nearest clump of bushes, and he grunted, replaced his cap over his eyes, and lay back to rest again.

He became aware of the footsteps at the same second they stopped, and he heard a hiss of indrawn breath. He lay motionless, pretending to be asleep.

"George! There's a man over there." A whisper.

"I can see that. So what? He's asleep. Come on." George's voice was low, too.

"But he's bare naked!"

"He's not—he's wearing underpants."

"Aye, and his bonnet." The girl giggled. "What's he doing?"

"He's sleeping, that's all, and it looks like he's been drying his clothes. He might've fell in the river. Shall we wake him up and ask him?"

"George, you're crazy. Let's slip around behind him."

"Why? He's asleep. We'll just keep walking."

"But what if he wakens?"

"What if he does?"

"He'll see us!"

"So what? He's the one with no clothes on."

He could hear them approaching slowly, coming within a few feet of where he lay, and as they approached their voices sank even lower. He didn't move.

"Look at the fancy smokes!" George's voice.

"What kind are they?"

"Don't know, never seen them before. Let's pinch a couple. He'll never notice."

The girl giggled softly. "You're daft, d'you know that? You don't even smoke." A pause, then, "Come on, George, let's go before he sees us."

"Okay, scaredy, but he wouldn't know who we were."

"He might, you never know. Come on."

He continued to lie motionless with his eyes closed until the sounds of their movement die away. Another minute passed and then the girl's laughter came to him from far away. He jack-knifed erect and dressed quickly. He closed his open tin of cigarettes, slipped it back into his jacket pocket, then he picked up his binoculars and strode off along the path after the young couple. He was walking fast, but he was in no particular hurry. He knew where they were going; they had been there before. He reached a dip in the path and stepped off into the undergrowth, heading up a gentle hillside.

On the crest of the hill, the undergrowth gave way to a massive stand of beech trees. He went over the crest and down the other side, still walking at the same steady pace. He heard the girl laugh, far off, and he lengthened his stride. The beech trees petered out and he came down off the hillside into a small valley. He ducked across a footpath and made his way up the other side of the narrow valley.

This gully was more hospitable than the one he had been in earlier. The slope on his side was fairly steep but heavily treed, and he angled his way toward a dense tangle of deadfalls. They had been there a long time and were thickly overgrown with moss and bracken ferns rooted in the rotting wood. He made his way into the middle of the tangle, to where the ferns were flattened and trampled, and there he took off his trench coat and spread it out over the trunk of a big tree where he could lean against it and support his arms while focusing his binoculars on the small footbridge that sagged into the river. Thick clumps of ferns grew under the bridge, springing out of a spongy mattress of needles. He put down his binoculars, took out his cigarettes, and checked his pocket watch. It was 3:55.

About five minutes later, he saw movement below him and froze. Two men emerged cautiously from a massive clump of rhododendron bushes, their eyes scanning the woods ahead of them. One of them stretched his arms above his head, and the Censor saw that he clutched a pair of binoculars. The second man had a pair, too. It never occurred to the watching Censor that they might be ornithologists. They were peeping toms, voyeurs.

The hidden Censor watched them dispassionately. Panty-watchers were a fact of life in rural Scotland. High illiteracy rates, record-breaking unemployment, a dearth of entertainment other than football and two BBC Radio stations, and a repressive, condemnatory attitude of dirtiness and shame attached to all forms of sexuality meant that otherwise normal, healthy, unemployed men sought relief from the tedium and frustration of their lives anywhere it could be found. And it could always be found in the hidden glades and woodland trysting spots young people sought out to court one another far from the judgmental eyes of their families and neighbours.

A flash of colour high up on the opposite side of the river caught the Censor's eye and his heart jumped into his mouth. Slowly, very slowly, he raised his own binoculars and trained them on the spot where he had seen the movement. The two young people were there, but they had seen the two men below and ducked down out of sight. He was higher yet than they were, and so could still see them. He picked up the girl's face, the boy's hand curled unnecessarily over her mouth. Her eyes were wide with fright.

The two men below were chatting idly as they walked along the side of the hill, unaware of how close their vigil had come to paying off. Their voices drifted up to him, but he could not make out any words. He watched them until they were out of sight, then shifted his glasses back to the youngsters, who stayed where they were for another few minutes and then walked quickly towards the old footbridge, darting nervous glances all around them.

Even after they reached their own sheltered spot they were still nervous, and they stood close together, George holding his girl's hand while they both scrutinized the valley around them. At one point, the boy's eyes swept the hillside and stopped on the deadfalls, but there was nothing for him to see. The watching Censor had dodged down long before the boy's glance came anywhere near his hiding place. He forced himself to stay there, making himself comfortable against the bole of the big tree trunk and lighting another cigarette, which he smoked furtively, fanning the smoke constantly with his hand to disperse it before it could rise above the level of the fallen trees. He was trying hard not to get excited, breathing deeply and forcing himself to concentrate on the steady, remorseless browning of the baby-blue cigarette paper as the heat of the live tobacco coal consumed it. It took a great effort of will to remain there without moving until the cigarette burned itself out against the gold paper of the tip. He dropped it then, twisted around onto his knees, and raised his head steadily.

The young couple had finally relaxed and were sitting side by side on George's spread-out coat, concealed from view in all directions except the one from which they were being watched through high-powered German-engineered field glasses. George had his arm around the girl's shoulders and was kissing her. Her arm came up around his neck and they fell back. Her right knee was raised slightly, and the watcher trained his instrument on the hemline of her skirt. He was less than forty yards from them, and at such close range the glasses denied him nothing that was to be seen.

It took about half an hour for George to become brave enough to try sliding his hand up under the girl's skirt. She closed her thighs, imprisoning his hand in a warm trap before it could reach its objective, and George's hand stayed where it was, in delightful captivity. For the time being, he made no effort to push it farther.

By the time his gentle but persistent assault on Annie's modesty succeeded, it was rapidly becoming too dark to see what was happening in the hollow by the ruined bridge. The Censor could see clearly that the girl's legs were spread and her skirt was bunched up around her belly, exposing her bared thighs, but her thick schoolgirl's underwear was black or navy blue, and the increasing dusk made it impossible to see clearly.

And then she sat up quickly, as though startled, and pushed the boy's hand away, her whole bearing radiating fear and tension. In a matter of seconds they were up, had rearranged their clothes, and were walking away quickly, hand in hand.

Livid with anger at what he saw as the girl's perverse selfishness, the watcher kicked furiously at the ground as they increased their speed and began to run, and then he snatched up his trench coat and took off running down the bank. He took three leaping strides along the tilted surface of the ruined bridge and jumped across the four feet of water in the middle, landing heavily on the up-sloping mossy planking on the other side, close to the shallow depression where the young people had been just moments earlier. There was nothing to see there now but the flattened grass and a few fresh scuff marks.

His breath coming in wild gulps, he straightened up to his full height, glaring along the path they had taken. "Bitch!" he whispered, his voice tight, close to cracking, stifled by inchoate, snarling fury. "Cock-teasing bitch!" Then he shrugged into his trench coat, leapt onto the path, and ran wildly after them, his coattails flapping around him, binoculars still clutched in his hand.

He knew precisely where they were going. They had hidden their bikes in the same place before. It was almost fully dark when he got there, and he stood unseen in the shadows behind a tree at the side of the path, watching as they kissed each other goodbye. They took their time about it, and his breathing had almost returned to normal by the time they separated.

George headed east, the lights of his bike dropping out of sight down the hill almost immediately, and the girl turned hers around and, standing on the pedals, began to speed towards where the Censor waited under a tree right beside the path. She was pedalling flat out, her skirt flapping well above her knees and the lamp of her bicycle flickering wildly on the rough ground, when he jumped out at her, straight-arming her, bicycle and all, into the long grass and bushes beside the path.

Time and Tide

Here in Canada, everyone and his brother—and if desired, his sisters, cousins, wife, and in-laws—can go out during the fishing season and catch salmon wherever there are salmon to be caught, and all it costs them is the outlay for a fishing licence. In Scotland in the 1950s and '60s, Salmon Fishing (complete with capitalization) was the jealously guarded right and privilege of the landed gentry who owned the land through which the great salmon streams ran. Peasants and punters, the working members of the working class, were personae non gratae there, where well-off middle-class tourists paid large amounts of money, by the day, for the rights to fish from a narrowly defined stretch of riverbank. They had no rights to fish on the other side of the stream. Those were sold to other tourists. It was a lucrative sideline for the landowners.

I remember that when I was ten—halfway to being a man, as I once thought—I was invited, along with a convenient uncle, to go on a day-long salmon-fishing expedition to the River Spey in northeastern Scotland, about fifty miles from my home. The uncle in question was my father's brother, and he was a schoolteacher, and that line of work was the most likely reason for his unusual openness to treating a boy as an almost-equal. He was free, of course, of the constant demands of shift work and heavy drudgery that afflicted practically every other man around him, and was the only one who had spare time to himself, and the luxury of being able to enjoy it free of worry. He was unmarried, and he genuinely enjoyed children, and so he took me

under his wing for several years, nurturing me in a way no other man
in the family ever had before.

He had a very rich titled English friend, a baronet who had been his
best friend and roommate in university, and this friend once invited us
(I was included by serendipity) to join him for a day of his fishing holiday,
at his expense. It was red-letter day for me—the only time I ever fished
for salmon in Scotland—and my uncle actually caught one. I never forgot
it, nor did I ever forget the flamboyantly wealthy extrovert who was my
uncle's friend, and in consequence, years later when I heard a friend and
colleague being uncertain about the wisdom of taking his son fishing, I
remembered my experience and wrote the notes underlying this story:

"Thanks for lunch. It was just what the doctor ordered." Thompson
glanced at his watch, holding the door of the restaurant open as his
colleague headed out, nodding his thanks to the smiling proprietress
as he passed the cash register by the exit.

Out on the sidewalk, Erikssen glanced up at the lowering sky and
turned his collar up in a futile effort to protect himself from the
weather. "I assumed it must be," he said, smiling and falling into step
beside Thompson as they set off along Broadway. "You ate enough
for both of us. How d'you stay so thin?"

"Selective gluttony," Thompson said. "Veal parmigiana and a
spot of pasta with meat sauce on the side, and a small glass of vino
collapso. But that's all." He turned his grin on his companion. "You
were so horrified by what was on my plate, you ate the whole basket
of bread *and* all the butter with your minestrone. Then you did the
same thing again with your fettuccine Alfredo. Thank God the
waitress didn't refill the basket a third time when she brought your
dessert. I would have protested."

"I know," Erikssen sounded dejected. "I'm defenceless against
fresh bread and butter." A moment later they reached the junction at
Cambie Street and stopped to wait for the lights to change.

A solitary gust of wind, blustery and autumnal, swept up the
funnel of Cambie from the False Creek inlet below them and buffeted

them gently as they stood waiting. Thompson looked speculatively at the cloudy sky. In the distance beyond False Creek, on the far side of the inner harbour of Vancouver's port, the North Shore Mountains had finally shrugged off the shroud that had concealed them for the past few days and now looked festive, dappled with broad patches of bright sunlight and heavy clumps of cloud shadow, and that patchwork effect struck him again, as it always did when he suddenly became aware, as being both relevant and appropriate to life on the Wet Coast.

Vancouver was a predominantly grey place in winter, perennially drab and uninspiring. He had an English friend who insisted that was why the province was called *British* Columbia. Clouds were a constant, too frequently descending as fog, accompanied by deluges of rain, sleet, and sometimes heavy wet snow that quickly turned to grey slush. In short, it could be lethally depressing, all too often for unbroken stretches of days and weeks, and the natives were prone to suicidal urges.

Its saving grace was the miraculous effect of infrequent and always surprising reversals. That, Thompson had long been convinced, was what kept the city populated and remarkably upbeat. The surging, exhilarating effect of waking up one morning to bright sunshine and balmy temperatures was restorative beyond belief. A few consecutive hours of brightness granted catharsis to even the most hopeless souls and offered benefits comparable to the sacrament of confession, in that the soul was cleansed afterwards, the spirit renewed, past transgressions forgiven, and the future that stretched ahead was always brimming with golden promise.

The traffic lights changed and Thompson stepped off the curb, wondering, cynically, about the odds of more rain to fall before they reached the office. He glanced at Erikssen, crossing by his side. "What's the forecast for the weekend, d'you know?"

"Not sure. What I do know is I've got a problem this weekend. I promised to take my kid fishing."

"That's a problem?"

"It is this weekend, because it's forty-five bucks an hour each, and the fishing's the pits. A month ago there was a run of coho and chinook at the same time. People were catching their limit in an hour, two hours at the most. Now nobody's catching anything out there except pneumonia. But I promised Jamie we'd go fishing and he's really looking forward to it."

"So take him out anyway. Maybe you'll get lucky."

"Nah, it's not that simple." They reached the opposite curb and turned to cross Cambie Street just as the light there turned against them. A young woman in a light floral-patterned dress stood in front of them and they both glanced appreciatively at her, noting the pleasant shape of her calves and ankles and the attractive way the light breeze moulded her skirt to her thigh.

"The kid's fourteen, going on fifteen," Erikssen continued, "and he's right at that threshold where his parents will soon turn into embarrassments. He's a hustler, too, just like me—always with friends to see and places to be. So he'd be bored out of his mind in half an hour if the fish aren't biting, and I don't need the hassle of paying ninety bucks an hour just to watch my son hating the little time we have together. And yet at the same time it's a duty thing, you know? I mean, I want to spend time with my son, but I'm not at all sure he'll want to spend idle time—down time, blah time, boring time—with his father, y' know? Anyway, it's not like I have any workable options. I hardly ever get to see him any more as it is. I had to cancel out on the last couple of things we were supposed to do together, and that didn't do much by way of increasing his belief in my ability to keep a promise to him . . . Add that to the way things are going at work, with the big corporate push everybody's being so secretive about at head office, and this might well be the last chance I get this year to spend some quality time with him. Jesus, I hate that phrase. Why do I use it? Isn't that a bullshit, phony expression? *Quality time.* Time's time." He shook his head; a tight little movement that reeked of frustration. "Anyway, if I don't make it happen now, it'll be next spring before you know it and then I'll really be time-poor. Never occurred to me when I made the promise a couple of weeks ago that the salmon run would be over by the time we got there."

The woman ahead of them stepped off the curb as the lights changed, and they followed her, tacitly conspiring to make no attempt to overtake her, each privately enjoying watching the way she swung her hips. Thompson raised his eyes in time to catch an expression of frank admiration on the face of a man coming towards them, his gaze fixed on the woman so intently that he had to make a visible effort not to turn his head as she passed him, and in the split second before they, too, passed each other, Thompson saw the other man's eyes focus on him and flash with undisguised hostility. *Whoops,* Thompson thought, *I can look, but don't you look at me looking.* The woman turned left when she reached the sidewalk, and Erikssen and Thompson both accorded her the courtesy of a last glance as they walked straight ahead along Broadway.

"So," Thompson said, "just the two of you? This is a father and son thing?"

"Yeah, Tanya's taking the girls down to Bellingham Saturday for some shopping and then they're going to some kind of show on Sunday, strictly ladies only. That's why I thought it would be good for Jamie and me to get out of the house, spend some man-time together, and then take the girls out to dinner when they get back Monday evening."

"Then I don't see your problem. You haven't even got one. The kid won't care what you do, as long as he's got you to himself."

"Nah, you don't get it. He's my *son,* Tom. I've got to do something to get his attention, something impressive that he'll remember as special—something distinctive."

"*Distinctive?* That's crazy! Makes about as much sense as quality time."

Thompson was less than ten years older than Erikssen, but their lives had been very different. Thompson had married young, raised his family early—and mercifully without any of the problems so many of his friends had had—and was now a grandfather three times over and still three years shy of fifty. Erikssen was thirty-nine and had three children, the oldest of whom, a teenaged girl, was in her final year of high school.

"Hell's teeth, George," Thompson continued. "Look at it from the kid's point of view. He's got an old man who's the senior vice president of sales for a big company—that's distinctive by anybody's standards, but all it means to him is that his dad hardly ever has time for him. So any time you make to spend alone with the kid, just him and you, has a value to him that you're never going to understand. It won't matter what you do with the time itself."

Erikssen's face was clouded with doubt. "You think so?"

"Don't have to think. I know it." They reached the end of the block and turned onto Yukon, heading down towards the waterfront and feeling the breeze strengthen as they faced into it. "I only ever took my son fishing three times when he was growing up," Thompson continued, "and I'm talking about perch and jack pike—not even trout, let alone salmon. This was shallow lake fishing, in Alberta.

"The first time, he was five. We had driven up to Calling Lake, about a hundred miles north of Athabasca township, to visit a friend of mine who was teaching in the Indian school up there. They probably call it the Aboriginal school now, maybe even the Indigenous people's school, but I'd bet most of the locals still call it what it's always been called. Anyway, it was early in the afternoon, school still in, so too early to meet my buddy, and I stopped the car at an old wooden dock on the shore, just to look around, catch some sun, kill some time. There was a dead fish among the reeds just off the dock, a little perch, about the length of my hand, and seeing it reminded me I had my tackle box in the trunk, along with a little self-contained one-piece plastic rod and reel. It was a cheap and gimmicky one-size-fits-all kind of thing that never really caught on, and I'd never used it, but my wife had given it to me as a stocking-stuffer and I'd had it in the trunk ever since, meaning to try it out. I'd forgotten it was there until I saw that little fish. So I dragged out the tackle, scooped an eye out of the little fish, and stuck it on my hook.

"My kid's eyes almost fell out, and he looked like he might throw up when that eye popped out. But as soon as that thing hit the water, a big perch went for it. By the end of an hour we had about twenty really nice fish and that little guy was whipping the eyes out of each one we caught and popping them right onto his own hook. You know he still talks about that day? Still remembers every detail—even the distance we had to walk to find wood to light a fire to cook the fish. He never forgot it, and the whole thing happened almost by accident. If that little fish hadn't been floating there in the water, I'd never even have thought about fishing."

Erikssen frowned. "So what's your point?"

"Same as the point I want you to ponder. How are you going to judge the value of time—your time—to a kid?"

There was no traffic on Yukon Street, and they made their way across it, jaywalking diagonally towards the scarlet awning of their office building at the bottom of the hill as Thompson continued. "You can't compare kids' time to adults' time, George. They're two different animals. From two different worlds. For us, time is money. Everything's hustle, hustle, hustle. Run here, drive there, can't be late for this, have to meet with him. And it's all bullshit, because when the contracts are all signed and finished, we can never remember what all the rush was about in the first place. But in the meantime, because of that bullshit, our kids get relegated almost out of our lives, and we're the ones that lose all around. You ever hear that song 'Cat's in the Cradle'?"

An expression of almost ludicrous surprise spread over Erikssen's face. "As a matter of fact I have," he said, pausing in the act of reaching for the office's heavy front door. "Tanya actually made me listen to it last Saturday night. About a guy who never has time for his kid 'cause he's too busy making a living, and then suddenly he's old and the kid hasn't got time for him 'cause now *he's* too busy making a living. What made you think of that? Have you been talking to Tanya?"

"I thought of it because that's what we've been talking about since we left the restaurant. I used to sing that song a lot back in my pre-corporate days, when I sang for a living. I met the guy who wrote it, too, Harry Chapin. We both guested on the same TV show one day. He was promoting a new album and I was just promoting my failing career, and we ended up in the green room together waiting to go on. That was in seventy-five, seventy-six, about a year after the song came out. He told me he didn't just write that thing for fun. It came out of his hide, he said—his hide and his old man's—and he had bad dreams about it happening to his own son one day. He died not long after that.

"You hear songs like that once in a while and there's a part of you that knows, right there and then, that they have something special— they're really meaningful, way more philosophical than they have any right to be. Too much of the time, though, they don't even register on our radar, probably because we're examining the lint in our own navels too damn much to hear them." He looked Erikssen straight in the eye. "But pay attention to this one this time, my friend. Take your kid fishing."

Erikssen stood there wide-eyed on the threshold of the office building, gazing intently at Thompson, who reached out and pulled open the heavy, brass-embellished door to let Erikssen enter. As they walked into the reception area, the receptionist held out her pink message slips, one handful for each of them.

"Mr. Erikssen, there's a Mr. Sullivan upstairs waiting for you. Dolores had to go out, but she made him welcome before she left, and he's having a cup of coffee in the executive lounge. He's only been here about five minutes. And Mr. Ling called about the advisory board meeting tonight at six thirty. And the caterers will be here by three to set up your four o' clock reception for the minister and his aides . . . Excuse me." She picked up the telephone and went into her answering routine before placing the caller politely on hold and looking up again at Erikssen.

"Oh, and a Mr. Crittenden called." She peeled a yellow sticky note from her blotter pad, where she had left it prominently displayed, crushing it now in her hand and dropping it into the waste bin as she delivered the message. "James Crittenden? He said his wife's in New York this weekend and he wanted to know if you'd like to take your son sailing with him and his son."

Erikssen looked at Thompson, his face creasing into a smile.

"Sailing?" Thompson asked.

"Sailing." Erikssen looked suddenly relieved. "Crittenden's a mad bastard. He and I went to school together. He's got a forty-two-foot C&C racing yacht that he keeps in Ucluelet, but he tows a twenty-thousand-dollar Zodiac and the son of a bitch is crazy about fishing."

Thompson took his own thick pink wad of messages from the receptionist. "Looks like it's going to be great sailing weather," he said quietly. "Happy fishing, Bud. And don't forget to give thanks, wherever you think they're due."

Shānjī

I remember a gloriously hot summer day in 1951 or 1952. It was a Saturday, though, because the Saturday ritual was in full swing as my grand-uncle Michael, who had not yet retired from the coal mines, demonstrated his mastery of the Tom Sawyer technique that once gave me countless hours of incredulous delight at the gullibility of his old cronies, who fell for his hypnotic magic time after time, every Saturday of every summer.

The long lawn at the side of our house was separated from the once tree-lined mile-long avenue that led to the laird's manor by a thick, healthy hedge of some variety of elm that needed to be trimmed regularly. The last remnants of the laird's family had died years earlier, penniless and intestate, and the home fields had recently been confiscated and converted to council housing. Many of my grand-uncle's old cronies had moved into the new housing estates, access to which was the old avenue that led by the side of our house. That meant, of course, that all of them passed our house several times each day, coming and going.

On summer Saturdays, then, Michael would cut the hedge. At least, he would start to cut it as he waited for the first of his pals to come along. In those days, the great sport in Scotland, for everyone still limber enough to run and kick, was the lovely game that they called football but Americans called soccer. The older men, though, who had grown up between the two great wars, had been raised in the horse-racing tradition and were fanatical about their races. Every man carried the weekly racing form data folded up in his pocket and was totally conversant with the statistics relating to each horse in every race at that weekend's meets, referring familiarly to individual races by time and racetrack, as in "the two thirty at King's Park" or "the three o'clock at Hamilton."

Thus Michael would clip leaves until one of his friends came along, at which point, after acknowledging the fineness of the weather that day, he would ask the introductory question, "What d'you fancy in the two thirty at Such-and-Such?" Opinions would be exchanged, statistics compared and verified, and within moments, Michael would be examining his friend's newspaper, doing additional research while said friend continued clipping the hedge. Within the half hour, there might be six or eight others there, each taking his turn with the clippers until the job was done, while the conversation moved on from the races to discussion of all kinds of other things. There was never any alcohol involved, not even bottled beer, and the only available seating was the grass of the lawn, but the weekend was in full swing and all was right with the world.

That particular Saturday sticks in my mind because it was the day that one latecomer, Mickey Murney, arrived with the news that another of their number, Luke McCabe, had met with a grim accident. He had been out on one of the last large estates left in the area, crossing a patch of meadow with dense clumps of bushes scattered about, and had failed, somehow, to hear the approaching fox hunt. Luke had blundered directly into the path of a knot of hard-riding huntsmen and had been seriously hurt in collisions with at least three galloping horses, unseating their riders. Two of the riders had ended up in hospital beside him.

That triggered a discussion I never forgot, on the morality of "the Hunt" as the gentry's pastime was called, and of blood sports in general. It was Michael himself who ended it that day by offering his judicious, dispassionate opinion on the ethics of it all and asking his friends to think about which of two choices they considered to be the more worthwhile: to ban all hunting out of hand, or to acknowledge the remote possibility that it might be better, in certain cases, to kill an animal and mount it carefully, thereby preserving and arguably "protecting" it, or the memory of it.

Years later, and continents away, I thought of that story, which inspired this one.

Jefferson stepped into the room and cleared his throat discreetly. "Pardon me, sir, your cousin Henry is here."

"Show him in."

Before the manservant could move to obey, the man behind him shouldered him aside and stepped through the doorway. "I don't need to be shown anywhere, Oscar, in or out."

Oscar offered him no more than a brief glance by way of greeting. "I just saw my father's Daimler pulling into the driveway," he said. "So I knew it was you."

"That's absurd. How could you possibly have known that?"

"Because I can't think of anyone else who would have the crust to commandeer my father's favourite car with the owner himself still lying dead in the house. No one else would have the cold-blooded arrogance to show his indifference to common courtesy so blatantly. What do you want, Henry?"

His cousin feigned innocence. "What do you mean, *what do I want*? Your father's dead, Oscar. My Uncle Mordechai. I came to offer my condolences."

"Bullshit. You're here to gloat. Over what, I'm not sure yet, but I've no doubt I'll find out."

"That's rather harsh, isn't it? How long has it been since we last saw each other?"

"Not long enough. I'll ask you again. What do you want?"

Henry Appleton's lip curled in the half sneer that defined him. "Still carrying the old bitterness, I see. But it has been sixteen years. Is it utterly inconceivable to you things might have changed since then? That *I* might have changed?"

Oscar eyed him speculatively. He had been holding his whiskey glass when he stood up, and now he sipped again at the vintage

Kentucky bourbon it contained. He leaned back against the table's edge and crossed his arms.

"I suppose not," he mused. "*Some* things have been known to change ... from time to time. However, a person can't outgrow assholery, Henry, and you were born an asshole—the most devious, treacherous, untrustworthy, obnoxious asshole I have ever known. In some ways—highly important ways—you're more like a machine than a living man. A mindless, soulless counting machine, a processor of financial data without a trace of genuine humanity or compassion in your nature. Now vomit up what you came to tell me, and then get out of my house."

Henry and Oscar Appleton were first cousins and fourth-generation industrialists in the traditional sense. Their paternal great-grandfather, Phineas Appleton, a Bible-thumping Scots Presbyterian, had built a formidable conglomerate of successful companies almost accidentally. He didn't care, at the outset, what kind of companies he bought, but he was fascinated by the dedication that was called for in their acquisition. An early investor in railroads, Phineas profited hugely with the completion of the Transcontinental Railroad, having long foreseen the overwhelming potential of the transportation industry, and by the time he was ready to retire, after almost four decades, he had absorbed enough practical knowledge of global commerce to organize his acquisitions into homogeneous groups of operating divisions that generated uncountable amounts of cash.

He had passed a thriving young empire on to his bright-eyed twin sons, Luther and Calvin, under whose joint guidance the Appleton Group tripled in size within fifteen years and then quintupled that in the following twenty. Calvin had an affinity for exploiting natural resources, and was attracted to any venture that was concerned with agriculture, carbon fuels, fur trapping, forestry, or fisheries. His brother Luther, on the other hand, was happy to leave Calvin to his preferred tastes, while he himself concentrated on shipping by land and sea, telegraphy, and road building. The ever-accelerating demand for transportation, of goods and people, and for industrial manufacturing in general were all grist for his never-tiring efforts.

Calvin and Luther brought the same enthusiasm to the group that their father had, and they prospered to the point where they were forced to split the Group's workload formally, with each of them supervising his own chosen area, coming together occasionally for the common good and to address the demands of increasing corporate oversight and regulation. Both men had married young, and married well, and each had one son and several daughters. Luther's son was Mordechai, and Calvin's son was Ichabod, and they were destined to assume their fathers' responsibilities.

It was in the fourth generation that things broke down. Mordechai's son Oscar and Ichabod's son Henry had been as different as chalk and cheese from birth. Theirs had been a mutual antipathy for as long as either one could remember, and their lives had been one endless fight for ascendancy. Ichabod himself had died young—most probably due to a surfeit of his acerbic wife Matilda, according to Mordechai—and Henry had taken over full command of the Group's Transportation Division early in his life, more than a full decade before Oscar came into his own with the Natural Resources Division. Now, unfortunately, Mordechai had died, leaving his position as chairman of the board vacant. And Oscar was more than certain that Henry had his eye on it. He would never miss a chance to further consolidate his power.

Now Henry raised his eyes and turned in a slow circle, examining the room, its decor and its contents. It lay directly off the front hallway and was obviously Oscar's domain, the central, private hub of his daily domestic activities. It was fashioned in the style of what had once been known as a gentleman's study: a solid, comfortably masculine room with that air of privileged, proprietorial luxury in furnishings and appointments found in the finest, most traditional men's clubs, and it reflected the rarefied and idiosyncratic tastes— some called them eccentric, while other designated them as simply weird—of its owner.

Oscar waited calmly while his cousin took silent inventory.

"I had heard you built this place," Henry said eventually. "Fleeing the family nest. I have to admit, it's quite impressive. Must have set you back a pretty penny. How many rooms do you have here?"

"Enough to accommodate the guests I choose to invite."

"Hmm. And which one is your favourite?"

"Which guest or which room? Ah, you mean which is my favourite room in the house. Why don't you tell *me*? I'm sure you already know."

For the first time, Henry looked surprised. "Why would I know that? I was only being curious."

For once, Oscar believed him. "Good," he said. "Then I'll show it to you. Come with me."

Oscar led Henry from his study into the palatial foyer, then past the grand staircase of snowy marble and along the wide, sunlit hallway beyond. The entire right wall there was made of reinforced glass, fronting the driveway and the sculpted gardens outside, and Oscar smiled to himself as he saw his cousin lean slightly closer to take particular note of the thickness of the glass, no doubt wondering whether the entire stretch of windows might be bulletproof. Henry had to lengthen his stride to keep up as Oscar walked straight towards a set of solid double doors at the far end of the long passageway. These appeared to have been carved from solid slabs of some exotic wood, and there was a small brass plate on each of them, one engraved with a Chinese script, the other reading *Shānjï*. Oscar waved his cousin inside.

Henry stopped just inside the door, leaning back to peer at the inscription. "What do these mean?"

"That this room has a name. That's why it's my favourite."

Henry looked around, frowning. "What's so special about it?"

"There's more to it than meets the eye," Oscar said.

"There's nothing to meet the eye at all. It's empty."

"Come now, Henry. You're supposed to be the great analyst of all things quantifiable. Analyze, then, why this should be my favourite room. If you can."

The room, some sixteen feet wide by perhaps thirty long, was windowless and oddly claustrophobic. The wall to Henry's right, almost within arm's reach of the doorway, was apparently the exterior wall facing the garden. The entire space was barren. Sumptuously barren, though, for the carpeting was of pure cashmere wool and the walls were panelled in polished burled maple. Nonetheless, there was not even a solitary stool to break the sterile lines, or a light fixture to focus on. Henry stood stock-still, his eyes moving constantly until he tensed slightly, then moved directly to the far wall, the dominant feature of the room. He peered at it closely.

"Are these plants real?" he asked, craning forward.

"As real as you are. They're mostly succulents, and I look after them myself . . . a kind of hobby."

The wall was made of rugged stones, bulky and awkward, uneven in depth and jagged-edged like newly created volcanic rocks. But between the stones, covering most of the rock face, tiny plants grew everywhere, ranging from thick, lush mosses and small clumps of succulents interspersed with brightly coloured flora to alien-looking tufts of scraggly grasses, some of which looked old and sere despite benefiting from the barely visible seepage of water that kept the face of the wall moist.

Henry spent long minutes staring closely at the wall, peering at it from all directions and touching a particular plant from time to time. Then he turned to his cousin. "You're fucking mad," he said icily, not even trying to keep the triumph out of his voice. "Batshit crazy. You're no longer fit to run the conglomerate. This . . . this *frippery* is proof of idle, feckless incompetence."

Oscar smiled serenely. "Move aside," he said. He leaned forward and did something to one of the smaller rocks, which moved with a barely audible click, and then he pushed gently with an index finger, and the entire wall swung sideways slowly and smoothly, revealing an identical room on the far side.

Henry swung to face his cousin, open-mouthed, and Oscar cut him off before he could speak.

"Now go in there and try again to answer the question. You can look, but touch nothing. There are cameras covering the entire space, and every move you make, every sound you cause or emit, will be recorded." Oscar followed Henry into the second room.

"But it's identical," Henry said, almost spluttering. "It's a copy of the same room."

"Not an exact copy. There are differences. It's up to you to find them and analyze them."

Henry glanced around. "Well, obviously, that thing." He pointed at an exotic black-and-gold bird that sat atop a flat rock high up on the wall, close to the ceiling. "What the hell is it?"

"It's a pheasant."

The bird perched proudly, peering out as though it were alive. Cascading like a silky waterfall, its incredible tail feathers stretched almost to the floor, highlighted in some places and hidden in others by the varying textures of the plants covering the nine-foot-high wall of rocks.

Henry gazed at it a moment longer, then grunted, his mouth quirking in what might have been a grimace. "It's not like any pheasant I've ever seen."

"No, this one's special. It's called a Reeves's pheasant, and it has the longest tail feathers in the world. That's something the like of which you've never seen, and couldn't imagine, Henry. Those feathers grow about a foot longer every year, and that one's tail is just short of nine feet long. It might be a world record, for both length and age, but we'll never know, because there aren't that many of these birds around, and zoo specimens don't signify scientifically because no one really knows how long the birds live in the wilderness."

"I'm not surprised, if people like you are shooting them. You built this wall just to show it off, didn't you?"

"No, I built it to enhance the bird, and to highlight its astounding camouflage. It's practically invisible, sitting up there, until your eye adapts to those textures in and among the rocks, and then you can't help but see it and be awed. And I didn't shoot it, Henry. I trapped it and brought it home, then looked after it until it died naturally, more than a year later."

"You *trapped* it?" Henry scoffed. "And where was that? In what people used to call Darkest Africa?"

"No, in a coniferous forest in the mountains of northern China."

"So, the sign on the door . . . ?"

"Is the bird's name, the Chinese name for Reeves's pheasant. It's pronounced *shan-chiyee*."

"And you travelled all the way to China to *trap* it? My God, that must have cost a fortune. It's insane. Did you trap anything else while you were there?"

"I did. I captured some lucrative contracts. Don't ever presume to lecture me about what I do with my own money, Henry. I won't be impressed . . . especially when the lecture comes from a ghoul who slaughters entire herds of wildlife every day, for *business reasons*, simply because their migratory patterns interfere with whatever right-of-way concessions he might be dickering over at that time."

Henry was quiet for a moment, then said, "I must admit, though, it's an impressive bird. The gold and black pattern of the feathers is really exotic. And the white raccoon-style mask is distinctive."

"It's not just impressive, Henry. It's stunningly, indescribably beautiful. One of nature's most superb works of art."

"And that's why you killed it."

"I told you, it died naturally."

"In a cage!"

"Yes, in a cage, and because of that, it's preserved exactly as it was in life."

"Where only you can see it."

"For now, yes. But when I'm gone, it will be on permanent display at a natural history museum, to astound people with its beauty. Had I not gone to China and brought it here, it would have died somewhere in that forest last year, or even before that, and rotted into nothingness without any wide-eyed child ever seeing the glory of it."

"Hmm."

This room had one piece of furniture, a two-foot-by-three-foot waist-high table, lacquered in gold and black, reminiscent of the pheasant's body feathers. On that table was a book, an eight-inch-thick album, covered in embossed leather.

"What's in the book?" Henry said.

"Photographs. It's a record of the expedition."

"May I look?"

Oscar shrugged. "Go ahead."

Henry began to leaf through it, scanning the photographs mounted four to a page and covered with protective film. They chronicled the project, beginning with the unloading of equipment from a freighter in Shanghai, then taking the viewer through the standard government-sanctioned tourist sites. The content changed radically, though, once the expedition was properly under way, and showed the terrain the group—a surprisingly large one—was travelling through. Eventually the number of photos to a page was reduced to two, and after that came a series of full-page informal studies of individual people, animals, and exotic birds, taken mostly within or close outside the expedition's evening camps.

Henry's desultory scan stopped abruptly, and he gazed more closely at the man in one picture. "I know this fellow," he said. "Who is he?"

"Who *was* he, you mean. His name was Sorenson, and he died about five years ago. He was a State Department spook—faceless, with an ultra-low profile. Worked with and for Winston Lord, one of only three Americans to attend the Beijing Summit with Mao in seventy-two. He was one of Lord's assets in arranging Nixon's visit."

"And why is he here, in this picture?"

"You mean in my camp? That's classified information, Henry. You don't need to know anything about that."

Henry kept turning the pages, then froze, staring at another photo. "That's . . ."

"It is indeed. And that's classified, too, so whisper if you name him."

"But—" Henry cleared his throat, then began again, whispering urgently and patently struggling to keep the awe out of his voice. "You actually met Mao?"

"Of course. How else could I have closed those contracts? I invited him for dinner, and he came."

"But—came to where?"

"To where we were, in the north. He flew in for a day."

"Good God!"

"God wasn't there, Henry. Mao was a Communist but he ruled an empire, and he was just as inclined to look after his own interests as any other emperor ever was. Bluntly put, he and I improved on Caesar's *veni, vidi, vici*. In this particular instance, we both came, we traded, and we both won."

"That's obscene—" Henry began.

Oscar cut him off with a chopping movement of his hand. "Enough, Henry! Spare me the phony outrage and the mealy-mouthed make-believe horror at the thought of my having anything to do with a Communist regime. It's time to stop with the bullshit. You've just proved your incompetence again. You're incapable of analyzing anything you see that doesn't have a visible price tag, and I know exactly what you're thinking."

Henry was frowning slightly now. "And what, precisely, do you mean by that?"

"I mean you're lying through your teeth about being scandalized, and you're really going cross-eyed with greed at the thought that you now have ammunition—those photographs—to use against me with the board of governors when you accuse me of incompetence and of fraternizing with our country's enemies. Are you really that naive? Do you really think any of your competitors wouldn't kill to gain access to the China market?"

He moved to the table and laid his hand flat on the album's closed cover. "Analytical observation, Henry," he said. "You have blind spots." He tapped the book's cover. "All you saw, from the moment we came in here, was this album, and yet you avoided it completely.

Sure, the pheasant is beautiful, but appreciation of beauty, per se, has never been one of your priorities. And yet this book, obviously valuable, was right here and you didn't look at it. Not once. You didn't even glance at the table it's sitting on, and yet that's where the key is."

"What key? You've lost me."

"The key to undoing all the shit you've been working on for the last ten months, ever since you found out about these photographs. You must have been surprised when Jefferson met you at the door this morning instead of your spy, Heddington. Heddington embarrassed himself some time ago by pointing a camera at proprietary property while he himself was being observed by a carefully concealed security camera above his head. We watched him after that, until he passed his information on to you. It was a simple matter to convince him to acknowledge the error of his ways and make himself invisible thereafter. He left quite suddenly, extremely well paid but without a reference, and he probably forgot to inform you.

"Since then, of course, you've been planning to expose me as a spy for the Chinese government, painting a very different picture of what happened on my Oriental trip. You want to make it look as though I was selling industrial and political secrets instead of setting up mutually beneficial trade deals." Oscar smiled, and enjoyed seeing the look of fear on his cousin's face. "But here's where it gets awkward for you. That *other* man you recognized? Sorenson? I told you he was a State Department spook, and he was. But so were all the other people there. The six top-level spooks you *didn't* recognize. Do you really expect to convince a grand jury or a House committee that they're all spies, too, Henry? You're in way over your head here, Cousin, and the proof's right here, in this drawer."

Oscar pulled open a drawer that had not been visible before, took out a sheaf of photographs, and handed them to Henry.

Henry fanned them in his hand, then stood with his head cocked, staring down at them. "I don't understand," he said.

"I know. But what does that look like to you?"

"It looks like me, photographed three times with different men, none of whom I know."

"Well, I won't bother you with names, but all three of those men are security personnel with foreign governments—China, Russia, and North Korea."

"That's ridiculous! I've never even seen any of these people before."

Oscar smiled. "I know that, Henry, and you know it. But no one else does." He nodded towards the fanned photographs. "The prints you're holding are just copies. The originals are untraceable and unfindable, but all too easily duplicated. They were very carefully engineered, Henry, using the latest techniques. Very convincing, wouldn't you say?"

He paused to let that sink home. "Besides, do you really believe the State Department was paying no attention to my going over there and meeting with Mao in person? Or had you simply forgotten to think that through, believing I was dumb enough not to have covered my tracks? What was to happen after you told your tale to the board of directors? Did you think it would have died there, unrecorded?"

As Henry opened his mouth to respond, Oscar cut him off. "And here's another notion for you to gnaw at, in the light of all I've said to you in the past few minutes: what do you think the odds might be that anyone in power will believe your version of this story when the consequence involves a massive risk of destroying our own intelligence efforts by questioning the motives of the very best people our country can provide for such specialized work?"

He quirked his mouth into a wry grin. "You're screwed, Cousin. No matter how hard you try to take the moral high ground, it's never going to wash, and everyone who knows you and hears about this will know you set me up and would have had me on my way to prison for treason if I hadn't caught on. So be realistic in sizing up the odds against you. You set me up for a hard fall—and I wasn't surprised. After all, you're the one who taught me, way back before we ever sprouted beards, never to trust you in anything. I forgave you for so many dirty tricks that you must have thought I was mentally defective. But eventually I came to see that you were the defective one, Henry. So not only have I never trusted you since that time, but I've trusted no one associated with you, either.

"My staff knew when Heddington first started working here that he had formerly worked for you, though neither of you said a word about that. So they were paying attention when he first wandered in here, during some carefully staged 'ongoing' renovations, and saw these pictures. And they were watching later, when he came back with a camera. We knew what he would do with the shots he took, and we were ready for whatever you would attempt."

"That's entrapment!"

"Bullshit. It's due diligence and self-defence. Since that first day, my people have documented every step, every false allusion, every penny you've spent, and every character assassination you've undertaken in building up your nasty little vendetta. Give your head a shake, Henry! This isn't the first time you've taken a run at besting me. And it's highly unlikely to be the first time you'll succeed. You'll never beat me this way, Cousin, no matter who you suborn or how much you pay."

Henry smirked. "You know, Oscar," he said, "I always thought you were mad—living alone, going on your weird trips and dragging home God knows what bizarre souvenirs, throwing your money around the way you do. Frankly, you've always been a bit of an embarrassment. We grew up in the same family, with the same privileges, the same ambitions. But for some damn reason, you think you're better than me, and you always have. Truth be told, you want absolute, total control of the Group just as much as I do. We both want the same thing: money."

Oscar shook his head. "It's not the same thing, Henry. Not at all. You seem to want money for its own sake. But you already have more money than you know what to do with, so why would you want more? It's probably the same sort of urging that drove you to take my father's Daimler this morning instead of one of the ordinary cars. It's an ego thing, a marker of your status, your importance. You just have to prove that you can't be beaten by anyone, in any game."

He took the photographs back, returned them to the drawer. "I'm sure you know what the old Romans used to say about money. *Radix malorum est cupiditas.* The love of money is the root of all evil. Well, they weren't far off the mark. Money can buy pretty much anything, but it can't buy integrity, and it can't buy justice. Nor can it, by itself, without help, create or sustain beauty. And it can't make a genuine human being out of an automaton like you.

"I don't want to take away what you already have, Henry, but I also don't want you to grasp any more power than you own by birthright. You will not force me out of the Group. So. Your choice is clear. Go directly to jail for conspiracy, without passing Go, or get the hell out of my house, my life, and my business affairs and don't ever think of coming back. The lawyers will take care of all the details and you needn't lose anything you've had up to this point.

"And you can forget about taking the Daimler when you leave here. Go straight to the airport or wherever else you're going. And stay away from the house—*my* house—from now on. That includes tomorrow's funeral services. I'll have your luggage shipped to you in Memphis. I will never see you, or speak to you, again." He pressed a button on the rocky wall, and in a moment Jefferson appeared.

"Call a cab for Mr. Appleton, James," Oscar said, "then show him to the foyer and stay with him until his taxi arrives."

Yesterday's Battles

This story is an homage to a man called John Robb and his wife, the quintessential memsahib whose first name I never knew, who were rejected from the British Raj and pensioned off with the rest of their contemporaries in 1947 when the viceroy, Lord Mountbatten, returned India to the Indians.

As a boy and the close friend of their adopted orphaned nephew, I was often in the Robb home during the early 1950s, and I always loved its atmosphere: a blend of exotic spice- and incense-rich aromas and outrageously beautiful objets d'art *arrayed in a flamboyant shrine to the former limitless wealth of the Indian Empire, yet simultaneously a temple for the worship of the quasi-religious belief system that, to its adherents, was the British Indian Army.*

Time passed, and I grew up, moved away from Scotland to England, and eventually forgot all about the Robbs and their memorable home. I remained oblivious to any memory of them for more than sixty years, until I formed a friendship a few years ago with a neighbour who told me this story of his own post-retirement separation pangs after a distinguished service career, when he was pensioned off as a general officer in the Canadian Armed Forces.

The association of ideas that his story sparked in my mind was immediate, and its connection to the long-forgotten memory of John Robb triggered an intense range of reactions: the ritual purging of a lifetime of memorabilia dedicated to bygone times and glories, and the inevitable, intrinsic regret of losing so much power after decades of working to achieve it.

My neighbour and John Robb, half a century apart, each served his own army in his own way, and each worshipped that army's gods. And each of them, in turn, purged himself of the same loyalty to a command structure and a way of life to which they had, with the inevitability of age, become irrelevant.

Matthew Hayden pulled off and stopped just inside the sagging battered gates by the side of the gravel road before reaching to switch off the engine. Instead of turning the key, though, he let the engine idle as he sat gripping the smooth plastic of the steering wheel, stroking it with the ball of his thumb and gazing out through the deluge of rain at the bleak place he had entered.

Directly ahead of him, the rusting pile of a huge industrial building was an unsightly scab against the jarring ugliness of the enormous yard surrounding it. Hayden sniffed, seeing the outlines of the place blurred by the liquid, swishing arcs of the wipers labouring across his windshield. The vast expanse of oily, puddle-scattered dirt fronting the building held no greenery; every trace of plant life had long since been ground into nothingness by unrelenting truck wheels.

It was pragmatism that had brought him here for the second time in a week, he told himself. He almost believed it, too. Part of him, the military part, grudgingly approved of the logic that had directed him to come, because it all made perfect sense; there were valid reasons for getting it over with once and for all. It was, he had convinced himself, the right thing to do—the only thing, in fact. And yet . . . His mind dredged up one of his all-time favourite observations from *Hamlet*: "Aye, there's the rub."

He inhaled sharply, sat up straighter, then eased the gear shift into Drive and crept slowly up to the vast building's yawning rusty doors, watching the windblown rain lash the dirty brown puddles and keeping an eye peeled for potholes and ruts. He would make his move, he decided, as soon as the downpour slackened. He shifted into Park, switched off his wipers, and sat waiting for the thunder of the falling rain to abate.

When he had come here the previous Sunday, there had been a scattering of dilapidated metal trolleys just inside the high entrance doors, obviously kept there to make it easier for people to transfer cargo from their cars into the main building. When the rain dwindled to the level of mere nuisance, he climbed out and walked gingerly through the enormous doors, trying vainly not to get mud on his shoes. Once inside, though, he stopped in his tracks again, no less awed this time around than he had been the first time he saw the place.

It was a municipal recycling depot, the only one in the city. As big as two or perhaps even three football fields, it held quite literally mountains of garbage, though he knew that, strictly speaking, *garbage* was the wrong name for the stuff. It was all recyclable material; everything under the vast, arching roof was reclaimable in one fashion or another, and reusable, or *repurposeable*, as he had heard one city bureaucrat claim—household appliances, construction debris, batteries of all descriptions, electronics, wiring, cans and bottles and plastics. Garbage, on the other hand, was landfill, pure and simple—hyper-sophisticated compost.

In one corner of the vast space, almost as far from the main doors as it could have been, was the enormous pile of scrap metal Hayden had come looking for. It contained more kinds of scrap metal than he had ever seen: black iron gas piping and aluminum scaffolding pipes; rusting, corroded drain pipes; rolls and scraps of silvery conduit; battered sheets and tubes of ductwork; old plumbing fixtures and some that looked brand new and usable. Ancient, dulled kitchen knives, flatware, and all kinds of cooking utensils, from heavy pressure cookers to rusted saucepans. The one metal conspicuously missing from the pile was copper, too valuable to throw away.

A sudden silence told him that the hammering of pouring rain above his head had stopped. He returned to the open doors to be sure, then quickly selected two of the sturdier-looking metal trolleys and pushed them out one by one into the cool afternoon air, directly to the rear gate of his vehicle, where he popped the lock and bent forward to reach inside.

There were six carefully taped and numbered plain brown boxes in the well of the Grand Cherokee, each two cubic feet in size. He had purchased them from a moving company and had been loading them carefully for several weeks. They were all hefty, but none of them was too heavy for him to carry alone.

Once they were safely transferred from the Jeep to the rickety trolleys, he closed and locked the rear hatch, then wrested the trolleys back into the depot, careless now of his muddied shoes. Taking two trips, he manoeuvred each trolley directly to the scrap metal pile, and when they were side by side he used a penknife to slit open the tape sealing the box labelled "#1." He folded back the flaps, feeling a strange constriction in his throat as the dim light of the overhead sodium lamps picked up the warm, yellow glow of what lay inside.

He reached in and withdrew the uppermost item, hefting it gently, almost lovingly, his eyes caressing it before he lobbed it up and away from him to strike a projecting length of iron gas pipe with a brazen clang and clatter down to the floor, where it vanished from view. He stood motionless, gazing at the spot where it had vanished, then repeated the ritual until the box was empty, hefting the solid weight of every piece before throwing it into the scrap pile.

Almost abstractedly, he flattened the empty box into a rectangle and weighted it with a piece of scrap metal before opening the box labelled "#2" and repeating the procedure, lobbing each of the pieces it held onto the now visibly gleaming pile of yellow metal in front of him. He thought it looked like a leprechaun's treasure chest from which the wooden sides had rotted away, leaving only the precious yellow gold.

"'Scuse me, if you don't mind my askin', but what's going on 'ere?"

Hayden had not been aware of being watched, but now he turned to see not one but two men standing close by, eyeing him curiously.

He thought they might work there, for they wore yellow canvas coveralls, scuffed steel-toed workboots, and regulation hard hats emblazoned with the universal recycling logo. The one who had spoken was clearly the senior of the pair, for the other seemed content to simply stand, empty-eyed, and let him do all the talking, stolidly chewing at a pink cud of gum, his mouth moving mechanically without ever closing. Hayden dismissed him, his eyes returning to the man who had spoken, and whom he had immediately thought of as Greek, from his voice, his burly physique, and the luxuriant moustache that masked his lower face.

"I'm sorry," he said. "Am I not allowed to be here? I thought this was a public facility."

"Well it is, kind of," the workman said in heavily accented English. "Leastways, this part is." He pointed towards a tatty old rope barrier that Hayden had not noticed. "That's what the rope is for—to stop people going into where is dangerous. Is a hard hat area there."

"So I shouldn't be here . . ."

"No, I din't say that. You're fine as long as alls you do is throw stuff over the rope. And that's exactly what you was doin' . . . except that it looked like gold."

Hayden merely blinked at him and the workman continued.

"Well, that's what it looked like at first, that you was gettin' rid of something valuable. Ain't that right, Karl?" Karl nodded, chewing his gum religiously, and the spokesman drew himself erect. "Except, it seemed to us you wasn't doin' it like you didn't want nobody to see what you was up to. Somebody tryin' to get away with somethin', he wouldn't wave it around like you was doin', one piece at a time, before he dumped it. It didn't make sense, what we was seein'."

"I can see how it would look that way," Hayden said. "You were exactly right. That's what I was doing—getting rid of something valuable, though valuable only to me, and not wanting anyone to see me doing it. Though you might not understand why." He hesitated, almost but not quite smiling. "I'm sorry you thought it was gold, though. It's just polished brass, nothing valuable."

"Why was it polished if you are going to throw it away?"

"Because I've been looking after it recently," Hayden said. "Though for years I had someone else to do that for me."

"Somebody died?"

"No. I retired."

The workman's eyes widened. "You *retired*? You're way too young to retire. What are you, fifty?"

"Fifty-three."

"Fifty-three, and retired. Sheesh! What the hell you did for a living, to retire at that age?"

"I was in the army. The Canadian Armed Forces." Hayden flicked a finger towards the trolley with its four remaining boxes. "And those hold all my memories. Souvenirs of thirty years of service, plus a few years as a cadet before that."

"Get out! You must've been just a kid, starting out."

Hayden acknowledged that with a tiny, almost rueful smile. "I was, but I always thought I'd been born late. I missed World War Two and Korea, so I really always felt I had no other choice but to sign up and do what I could, even if I was late."

"What's your name, then?"

Hayden raised an eyebrow. "Matthew Hayden. Why do you ask?"

"Curious is all," the workman said. "Stav Apostopolos, and this lump"—he indicated Karl with a sideways nod—"he's a Russian of some kind. Name you can't pronounce. Stav's short for Stavros. I'm Greek."

"I'm glad you told me that," Hayden said, straight-faced. "I might have wondered otherwise."

Apostopolos ignored him, settling his hard hat firmly in place and stepping over the rope to rummage among the items Hayden had thrown away. He straightened up after a few moments, holding an item in each hand. One was a broad two-inch deep ashtray made from the base of a heavy-calibre artillery shell and fitted with three raised shelves to hold cigars. The surface had been etched with the legend "To Lt. M. J. Hayden, from his Messmates at CFB Wainwright,

Alberta. Go slay dragons, Matt." The second piece was a brass plaque, mounted on a polished mahogany plinth, which read: "To Captain Hayden, from his Messmates at 2 Canadian Mechanized Brigade Group, CFB Petawawa, Ontario."

Karl popped a pink bubble, then yawned and wandered away, back to whatever job had been interrupted.

The Greek turned back to Hayden. "Well," he said, "you are who you say you are, so tell me." He waved towards the four unopened boxes. "These all contain the same kind of things?"

Hayden nodded.

"So what the hell's going on? Why you junk everything? That's like a lifetime of memories."

"It is."

"Then why?"

"Because I can't keep it. When I was serving, my wife and I lived in officers' housing. It wasn't luxurious but it came rent-free, all our food was taken care of, and we had plenty of room. And on top of all that, I had a servant, a batman we called him, to polish all my brass. RHIP."

"What's that mean?"

Hayden grinned. "Army bullshit. RHIP means 'Rank Has Its Privileges.' Were you ever in the army, Stav?"

"No, sir, I never was. Lucky, I suppose, though I don't really know if that's true or not . . . So, did you ever fight a war?"

Hayden shrugged dismissively. "No, not really. But I spent thirty years training for one. And then I retired. And my whole life changed. I was suddenly out on the street at fifty-two and facing the real world that ordinary civilians lived in. Couldn't afford a big house any longer, and the nicest one we could afford is way too small to hold all this." He waved a hand at the boxes beside him. "Besides," he added, "my wife's sick of it and doesn't want it in the house. It reminds her of the years we spent apart while I was active, and she's always hated the idea of an old soldier's 'I Love Me' room. So here I am, on a rainy Sunday afternoon."

"Damn," the Greek said, shaking his head. But then he looked again at the trolley and his eyes sharpened. "Can I ask you somethin' else?"

"Of course," Hayden said. "Go ahead."

"Is it important the boxes is all numbered? Does it mean anything?"

Hayden grinned broadly. "It probably means I'm obsessive-compulsive," he said. "It was a good trait to have in the army, but there's not much use for it in civilian life. But yes, it's important. I numbered the boxes in chronological order. The first two are all from my years as a subaltern—that's a junior officer—before I was promoted to captain. All the awards and presentation pieces were cruder and clunkier then, usually handmade in the garrison workshops, and somehow that made them more personal than the fancier pieces that came later."

He tapped the sealed top of carton #3. "Starting in here, everything relates to my career as a more senior officer: three boxes from my times as a captain, major, lieutenant-colonel, and colonel." He shrugged. "It's more of the same, really, but the rankings are all higher—not just my own but those of the people making the awards as well—and the postings are more significant in terms of building a reputation.

"As I climbed the ladder, they put me through more advanced training, trusted me with more and more difficult assignments, and gave me more authority. And so the contents of these last four boxes are richer and more substantial."

"Not so many brass ashtrays, then?"

For the first time in several weeks Hayden erupted into a deep belly laugh. "In the name of God, don't ever be tempted to think such a thing, Stavros. If there's one real constant in military life, it is that no modern army ever suffers from a shortage of brass, whether it's the old-fashioned type we used to use to make weapons or the blustering, moustache-twirling senior-officer brass, famous for stupidity and their obstinate refusals to accept anything new. Thank

God most of those dinosaurs are gone now, but the odd one still turns up occasionally."

He reached out and laid his hand on the nearest carton. "So these boxes are full of brass, too, but the brass in these is lighter. Brass plaques, engraved, wood-mounted, personalized." He opened up the next box and took out a plaque, held it out to Stavros, who took it with a nod and inspected it closely.

"You're right," the workman said. "It's fancier, but the brass is cheaper, thinner. If it's not important to you, it's probably worth less than the stuff you threw away already."

"You're exactly right, my friend," Hayden said quietly. "I've been having trouble getting my head around that notion—the ins and outs of it—but you've nailed it square in the centre. Apart from the memories all this represents, and those are golden, this is only cheap brass—genuinely worthless."

Apostopolos frowned mildly, then turned his head towards the sound of Karl returning with his lunch.

"So the last box," Apostopolos said with a grin, "must contain really cheap brass."

Hayden grinned right back at him. "Not quite," he said. "A general officer's memories, my friend."

"What is this, a general officer? He's different from a regular officer?"

"He is. He's senior management."

"General!" the workman said, awe suddenly evident on his face. "You were a general? How many stars?"

Hayden smiled again. "Generals don't have stars in Canada, Stavros. American generals have stars. Canadian generals have gold maple leaf emblems on their epaulets. I was a Canadian major general, and now I want to thank you."

"For what? I have done nothing."

"For bursting my bubble of self-pity," Hayden said. "For showing me it's what I did for those thirty-odd years that's important—not my own importance or my authority, and certainly not what I brought out of it, but the contributions I made. And I'm grateful. Would you do me one favour?"

"Of course."

"Leave me to finish this alone, if you will. It won't take long." He glanced at his watch. "My wife has been out playing bridge this afternoon and I'd like to be home when she gets back."

"Of course, General." He inclined his head. "Go with God."

Hayden returned to disposing of the reminders of his former life, which he did with the same steadfast deliberateness he had shown earlier. After he lobbed the last piece onto the pile he stood motionless for long moments, staring into nothingness. Then he drew himself up to his full height, turned crisply, and marched towards the exit.

He stopped just inside the doorway and turned back to the two workmen by the scrap pile. He raised a hand to wave, but it never reached shoulder height as he realized what he was seeing.

In the deepening shadows by the scrap heap, the two city workers were standing at attention, their right hands raised to their foreheads in their closest approximations of a military salute.

Hayden reeled a little, for in the strange half-light of the alien-looking chaos of the recycling depot, he saw things his rational mind knew were impossible.

On the front slopes and shoulders of the piled mountains of junk scattered everywhere, he saw human shapes among the shadows. Not quite recognizable, they were nonetheless familiar enough to cause him to crinkle his eyes and squint, trying to clear his vision even as his eyes teared up. On the sides and summits of the piles of rusting, discarded rubbish, hundreds of uniformed shapes, silhouetted against a dim curtain of pale, eerie light, seemed to be looking down at him, silent and motionless. He allowed himself to look back at them for a moment, sensing rather than seeing their diversity and oddly uniform differences, and recognizing the impossibility of what he was seeing. And then he closed his eyes and inhaled sharply, straightened yet again to his full but unimposing height, and opened his eyes.

The curtain of light had vanished, together with the silhouettes it had displayed. Only the two workmen remained, still standing at attention.

Matthew Hayden tried to stand up even straighter, though he was ramrod stiff already, and swallowed hard against the painful lump in his throat. And then he returned the two workmen's salutes with a perfectly executed one of his own. He held it for five measured seconds, then lowered his arm, performed a perfect military about-face, and walked out into the pouring rain and home to his wife.